THE CATACOMBS

The carousel spun silently and slowly, as if it couldn't get enough power to move at the right speed.

A teenage girl with short black hair rode by, draped over a wooden horse, her head lolling at an impossible angle. Dead.

Another girl rode by, clutching one of the horses that rose and fell, rose and fell in silence. Her skin was a bluish gray and her blue skirt dripped muddy water onto the wooden floor of the carousel. The girl stared straight ahead, her eyes flat and still.

A girl in a yellow summer dress, white gloves, and a white hat rode by next. Her body was slumped in a chariot seat, her mouth open in a silent scream of terror. Blood dripped from her throat.

TITLES IN THE POWER SERIES
by Jesse Harris

THE POWER

THE
CATACOMBS

by Jesse Harris

RED FOX

A Red Fox Book

Published by Random House Children's Books
20 Vauxhall Bridge Road, London SW1V 2SA

A division of Random House UK Ltd

London Melbourne Sydney Auckland Johannesburg
and agencies throughout the world

First published in the United States by
Alfred A. Knopf, Inc. 1992

Red Fox edition 1993

Phototypeset by Intype, London
Printed and bound in Great Britain by
Cox & Wyman Ltd, Reading, Berkshire

ISBN 0 09 922141 1

For Walter and Minnie Graham,
who gave me the world in a bag of books.

PROLOGUE

Somewhere in the dark tunnels of the Catacombs, a shadow moved. Decaying fingers with ragged nails trailed along the rock walls, sliding through occasional trickles of water. He was hungry. It had been too long since he last fed. Now he moved through the narrow passageway toward light, toward the entrance to the tunnel. He could already taste the living flesh he craved. It was only a matter of time. She was waiting for him – another young girl. He couldn't see her, but he could feel her fear. He could taste her blood.

The woman's eyes sprang open. He was awake again. And hungry. She could feel it. He was hovering in the Catacombs, far too close to the entrance, waiting.

She lumbered to her feet, not bothering to pull a robe over the tentlike nightgown that covered her massive body. She took six heavy steps across the trailer to the altar, where incense rose to the smoke-stained ceiling.

With a grunt she settled onto a bench and gazed down into the mirror that lay on the altar, letting her mind seek him.

There. She tried not to shudder as she looked at the strip of flesh that hung from his cheek, revealing white bone underneath.

'Hunger.' His voice rasped in her mind, though his death-ravaged lips didn't move. A drop of yellow pus oozed from the eye that protruded halfway from its socket.

'Soon,' she replied, sending the word with her mind. 'I've found one.'

'When?'

'Tomorrow. A young girl, a runaway. She's been hiding in the Tunnel of Love.'

He was silent for a moment. She could almost feel him weighing the options.

The huge woman's heart began to pound faster. He must never try to emerge from the Catacombs to hunt his own prey. He must never be let loose in the park. He must never emerge from the Catacombs. 'Of course, she'll still be alive when we bring her to you.'

The corners of his mouth arched in a grotesque smile. 'I'm waiting.'

Her heartbeat didn't begin to slow until he turned and began to move back toward his lair, gradually fading into the gray recesses of the mirror.

She and the others would have to get busy. . . .

CHAPTER 1

Lilith Caine closed her eyes and inhaled deeply. 'Mmm . . .' she said, 'cotton candy, peanuts, hot sausage sandwiches . . . don't you just love the way this place smells?'

'Lilicat,' said her friend McKenzie Gold, 'if you don't open your eyes, you're going to walk right into the ring toss.'

Lilicat's brown eyes popped open and she grinned. 'I can't help it,' she said. 'Amusement parks are the greatest. I mean, all the rides and the goofy organ music – don't you think this place is heaven?'

McKenzie wrinkled her nose as she gazed around the crowded midway of Idlewood Park. 'I can live with the organ music, but the rides – '

'I thought you were over your fear of

heights.' Lilicat shot her friend a concerned look.

'I wouldn't exactly call it "over," ' McKenzie admitted. 'Let's just say I've made progress.' She glanced at the Ferris wheel and something called the Demon Drop, looming before them. 'This time last year I probably would have run screaming from the sight of a Ferris wheel.'

'See?' Lilicat said optimistically. 'You *are* getting over it. By the end of the summer – after we've spent every day working here, meeting fascinating people, and being paid fabulous salaries – riding the Ferris wheel will be no scarier than brushing your teeth.'

'Dream on,' McKenzie said, but she hoped Lilicat was right. School was out for the summer, and neither of them had a job. They'd applied to nearly every restaurant and store in Lakeville and hadn't gotten a single offer. It had been Lilicat's brainstorm to fill out job applications at the amusement park. McKenzie didn't really believe that Idlewood would have fantastic job opportunities, but she couldn't afford not to check it out.

The sun disappeared behind a bank of clouds as the girls passed the long lines waiting for the roller coaster, and suddenly McKenzie felt uneasy. She looked up. Above them the cars on the track trundled to the top of the first hill. McKenzie watched as the first car came to the top of a sickeningly steep drop. Then she quickly turned away. It was her old fear of heights. Despite what she'd told Lilicat, it was a long way from gone.

Lilicat snapped her out of her daze. 'The Catacombs!' she said, pointing at a sign lettered in dripping red paint. 'Look, Mack, that's the new ride everybody's talking about.'

The sun burst from behind the clouds as McKenzie followed her friend through the crowds. Lilicat's vibrant pink overalls played up her dark, glossy shoulder-length hair and pretty features. McKenzie shook her head. She still felt uncomfortable, slightly dizzy, as if the ground beneath her feet weren't really solid.

The line for the Catacombs was even longer than the one for the roller coaster. McKenzie followed Lilicat to the front of the line so Lilicat could get a better look at the sign.

A little boy whined, 'Daaaaa-deeeee, they're cutting in.'

The young father frowned at the girls.

'Honestly, we're not,' Lilicat assured him. 'We're just looking.'

The sign read:

Visit the Catacombs if you dare,
What will you encounter?
Your wildest dream or your worst nightmare?
Only the path you choose will tell.

McKenzie shivered in the late June sun.

' "A different adventure guaranteed every time," ' Lilicat read aloud. 'It's supposed to be incredibly scary. I can't wait to try it!'

'Maybe we'd better see about jobs first,' McKenzie said, wondering why she felt so uneasy. After all, she was safely away from the roller coaster, and the Catacombs was just a fun house. Wasn't it?

'Right,' Lilicat agreed. 'Now where did the man at the gate say the personnel office was?'

Mack nodded ahead of them. 'Down at the end of the midway, I think.' Feeling a little queasy, McKenzie inhaled the scent that wafted from the food concessions, a mixture of hot dogs, hot sausage, and candied apples. 'If we get jobs here, we'll probably gain enough weight to work as fat ladies by the end of the summer.'

'Like you really have to worry,' Lilicat said with a laugh. McKenzie was taller and slimmer than her small friend. 'How about some cotton candy?'

A minute later McKenzie was picking at Lili-cat's cotton candy but not really eating it. That funny unsettled feeling had come back and her stomach was churning.

Something was definitely wrong. For as long as McKenzie could remember, she'd had a special sense. Sometimes it took the form of visions or dreams. Other times it was an uneasy feeling or sudden chills. Almost always it was a message about the future, often a warning. McKenzie swallowed hard. She was tempted to say, 'Lilicat, let's get out of here now.' But she didn't. There was some sort of danger at Idlewood; she could feel it. And she couldn't very well leave when someone might need her help. She really had no choice; she had to stay and find out what the problem was.

'Mack, while you've been staring off into space, I found the personnel office.' Lilicat pointed to a weathered booth down a small aisle off the midway.

Mack blinked as they entered the booth. A man stood behind the counter, his back turned. He was wearing what had to be the ugliest shirt she'd ever seen. He turned to face them and Mack realized he wasn't wearing a shirt at all; the 'print' was actually hundreds of tattoos. Two dragons sparred on his chest, sinking claws into each other's scaly bodies. The tips of the man's nipples were blackened to form the pupils of the dragons' eyes. Real and mythical animals cavorted over his arms and back in a riot of blues, greens, reds, and yellows. McKenzie tried not to stare. Lilicat, she noted, was looking intently at the counter.

The man grinned at them, almost as if he enjoyed their discomfort. 'May I help you?' he asked in strangely accented English. 'I'm Elijah, Tattooed Man and Head of Personnel.'

McKenzie bit back a grin. She'd met about a dozen personnel people in the last two weeks; Elijah definitely took the prize for Most Unusual. 'We'd like to apply for summer jobs, working the concession stands or the rides.'

The man looked them over. 'I'm sorry. No jobs. All our positions are filled for the summer.'

'Could we apply anyway?' Lilicat asked. 'Just in case someone quits?'

Elijah reached beneath the counter to his right. As he did, McKenzie saw, nestled in with the animals and abstract designs on his wrist, a skull that seemed to be leering at her. He set job applications and a couple of chewed-up pencils in front of the girls. 'You can fill out these forms. If we need you, we'll call.'

The girls filled out the applications, thanked Elijah, then headed back toward the midway. McKenzie turned to look back once. She shuddered. From this distance Elijah's tattoos were a hideous blur of colors.

'I can't believe it.' Lilicat brushed a strand of dark hair from her eyes. 'I was so sure we'd find jobs here. Idlewood must hire dozens of people! How could they not have two more measly little openings?'

McKenzie shrugged, secretly glad. She'd felt uncomfortable around Elijah, and still had her doubts about Idlewood.

'What now?' Lilicat asked glumly.

'Might as well have fun while we're here,' McKenzie replied in a deliberately cheerful tone. Lilicat knew about her special sense, but McKenzie had lost track of the number of times she'd ruined a perfectly good day by saying, 'Lilicat, I feel something strange here.' This time McKenzie was going to act like everything was normal and simply figure it out for herself.

They turned onto the main stretch of the midway again. As they neared a lemon-ice booth, Lilicat's face lit up. 'Mack,' she whispered, 'will you look at that guy over there!' She pointed at a slender dark-haired boy in jeans and a T-shirt who was joking with the booth operator.

'Nothing like a cute guy to get *you* over a disappointment.'

'Cute?' Lilicat said. 'Look at him, Mack. He's gorgeous! Kind of reminds me of Luke Perry.'

'If you squint a little,' McKenzie teased. 'He's looking this way. Go over and talk to him.'

Lilicat hesitated a moment and then shrugged. 'Why not? Can't hurt to try.'

McKenzie watched as Lilicat went over and asked a question; it looked as if she were asking for directions. The boy smiled down at her and said something that made Lilicat laugh. McKenzie decided to give them a few minutes alone.

She wandered along the opposite side of the midway wishing her boyfriend, Aidan, were with her. She glanced at her watch and sighed. He'd promised to meet them in the park at seven. Unconsciously, her fingers went to the crystal pendant she always wore, the one her Grandma Alice had given her. When she was a little girl, she'd believed the crystal was a magic stone that would protect her from harm. McKenzie smiled at the memory. It had been years since she believed in that kind of magic.

Still, there was something about the crystal's cool, familiar surface that was reassuring.

'Ho there, pretty miss,' called an old man in one of the game booths. 'Try your luck. Break a balloon, get a prize; break three balloons, get your choice!' McKenzie smiled at him and kept walking, but he didn't give up. 'Break nothing, win a prize!' he called after her. 'Everyone's a winner!'

McKenzie turned back, deciding she might as well play. Her eyes scanned the shelves of the booth and fell on an adorable stuffed zebra on the bottom shelf. She plunked down fifty cents, took three darts, and broke one balloon.

'A comb for your lovely auburn hair, miss.' The concessionaire handed her a comb as long as her forearm. 'Another try?'

'No thanks,' Mack told him. She wondered if she could get Aidan to win the stuffed zebra for her.

She circled back to where Lilicat and the Luke Perry look-alike were still talking. Lilicat turned, saw McKenzie, and waved her over. 'This is Tony Robards,' she said, her cheeks almost as pink as her overalls. 'My best friend, McKenzie Gold.'

Tony smiled, his teeth white in his tanned

face. He had warm brown eyes. 'I see you won the giant comb.'

McKenzie rolled her eyes. 'So much for my skill with darts.'

'Tony's father owns Idlewood,' Lilicat said. 'And guess what? Tony's the one who redesigned the Catacombs.'

'I didn't do it all by myself. Just came up with some of the ideas, that's all.'

'We can't wait to check it out,' Lilicat gushed.

'We can't?' McKenzie echoed, feeling slightly alarmed. Tony looked at her curiously and she explained, 'Lilicat and I have slightly different ideas about what's fun.'

'That's okay,' Tony said. 'Not everyone likes the scary stuff. How about a ride in the Tunnel of Love?'

'Sure.' Lilicat turned toward McKenzie. 'C'mon, Mack, we can fit three.'

McKenzie shook her head. 'Three's a crowd. I want to check out some of the other attractions, anyway.' She could tell Lilicat really wanted to be alone with Tony.

'If you're sure. . . .'

'Go on. I'll catch up with you guys later.'

Tony and Lilicat walked off talking. Neither seemed to notice the sticky lemon ices that had melted over both of them. Looks promising, McKenzie thought. It'd been a while since Lili-cat had gone out with anyone. Tony was hot, and he seemed really nice. Definitely promising.

McKenzie wandered down the midway past a duck-shoot, a test-your-strength game, and a pizza stand. She stopped outside the Skee-Ball arcade. The clack and roll of the balls almost drew her inside, but the place was packed. She'd come back later.

Ahead of her was a sign that read, 'What does your future hold? Find out for no charge from Madame Beaupree, renowned French psychic. Donations accepted.'

What a hoot, McKenzie thought. No real psychic would hang out a sign like that or call herself Madame Beaupree. Still, McKenzie couldn't help being curious about what this 'psychic' would be like.

Clouds of incense smoke hung in the tent. McKenzie could just make out a woman in a red velvet turban sitting behind a small table. Mack stepped in, letting the tent flap fall behind her. The woman stood up, her burgundy satin caftan swirling around her thin body. A jagged cigarette hole marred one of the flowing sleeves.

'Enter the tent of Madame Beaupree,' the woman said in a heavy accent. McKenzie bit back a smile. The woman was about as French as a French fry. Madame Beaupree nodded to a low stool on the other side of the table, and McKenzie sat down. 'Now, my darling, tell Madame what it is you wish to know.' The woman waved her long red talons through the air, watching McKenzie through narrowed, heavily made-up eyes.

McKenzie thought for a moment. The woman was obviously a fake. She wasn't about to ask her anything serious. 'Oh, tell me something about my boyfriend,' she said at last.

'The spirits will guide us, my child,' Madame Beaupree assured her. She whipped an embroidered cloth from the center of the table, revealing a surprisingly beautiful crystal ball.

Madame's eyelids dropped shut, and she passed her hands over the ball again and again, as if she were washing it. Meanwhile her body swayed, her torso going one way, head and neck the other. What a performance, McKenzie thought.

'Nothing,' the psychic said, sounding disappointed. 'I get nothing – '

McKenzie wondered if she was supposed to 'donate' something now. She was reaching into

15

her pocket when Madame Beaupree shrieked as if someone had pinched her. Startled, McKenzie dropped a dollar bill on the table.

Without missing a beat, Madame Beaupree's hand snatched up the bill and hid it somewhere in the folds of her caftan. 'Now the spirits speak. Now the voices of the dead talk with us. Now the departed arrive.'

The woman went into a total frenzy. McKenzie looked behind her, almost expecting to see some cadaverous creature lurking there.

Nothing but the closed tent flap.

Madame continued, a little louder. 'Now the voices of the dead – '

McKenzie wondered if she could get up and leave without Madame Beaupree noticing.

Madame opened her eyes and thrust her head close to the ball, gazing into it. 'I see it, my lovely. You will meet a tall, handsome, dark-haired man.' Her eyes flicked upward to McKenzie's. 'That's what you want, isn't it?'

McKenzie was about to tell her that she had a tall, handsome, blond boyfriend when a thin, dark-haired man who had to be at least seven feet tall bounded in, pointing to himself comically. He was so tall his head pushed at the top of the tent.

McKenzie laughed. 'He certainly is tall and dark-haired.'

Madame Beaupree leaped to her feet and shook her fist at the stranger. 'Get out of here right now, Stretchman.'

Despite his size, Stretchman looked like a little kid who'd been scolded. McKenzie couldn't help feeling sorry for him.

'What's going on, Stretch?' A dwarf in scaled-down Levi's and a black T-shirt slipped through the tent flap. 'Did she give some poor pigeon the old "tall, dark, and handsome" routine again?'

'Get out, Shorty!' Madame shrieked. 'And take him with you. How am I supposed to commune with the spirits if you two won't leave me alone?'

'You can't talk to us that way,' Shorty said in a raspy voice. 'If you weren't such an old hag I'd punch you in the schnoz.'

Madame Beaupree puffed up in indignation. 'You wouldn't dare!'

Shorty thrust his face into hers and said, 'Oh, yeah? Let's get out of here, Stretch.'

Looking like a sad hound, Stretch followed Shorty from the tent. As they left, Shorty's words drifted back. 'Tall, dark and handsome. Two out of three ain't bad, Stretch.'

17

McKenzie was about to thank Madame Beaupree and leave, but Madame grabbed her wrist and said, 'Wait! I see it now. Your senior prom, a pink dress, dancing . . . an engagement ring!' Her voice dropped to a hypnotic whisper. 'Look into the ball. . . .'

I'll never escape, McKenzie thought. Nevertheless she sat down and looked into the ball.

To her surprise she did see pink. But it wasn't a prom dress.

No. She leaned closer to the ball, looking into its depths. She saw a girl wearing some sort of pink outfit, moving around wildly. But the girl wasn't dancing.

She was fighting for her life! Struggling in the water beneath a big paddle-wheel, her dark hair tangled in the wheel. The girl couldn't breathe.

McKenzie couldn't see the girl's face, but she didn't have to. Lilicat was wearing pink today.

And she was in the Tunnel of Love.

CHAPTER 2

McKenzie rushed out of the fortune-teller's tent, not even bothering to push aside the tent flap. She stumbled over something low to the ground and then hurtled into a human telephone pole. 'Oh, it's you,' she said, staring up at Stretchman. She gazed down and flushed with embarrassment as she realized that what she'd stumbled over was Shorty. 'Sorry!' she apologized. 'But could you help me? Which way is the Tunnel of Love?'

As Shorty pulled himself to his feet, Stretchman pointed to the back of the park.

'Cut that out!' Shorty told him angrily.

The giant stared down at him in surprise. 'But Shorty, she needs help. She – '

McKenzie had no time to wonder about the odd exchange between the two men. She raced ahead in the direction that Stretchman had shown her, threading her way through the crowds.

'Hey, watch where you're going!' a boy yelled as McKenzie accidentally bumped him.

'Sorry,' Lilicat, Lilicat . . .

A scream split the air.

McKenzie raced forward, trying to ignore the painful stitch in her side. If she could only get there fast enough, she might be able to save her friend.

She pushed through the growing crowd at the entrance to the Tunnel of Love.

A girl hid her face against her boyfriend's chest while he looked down into the channel with something like disgust on his face. 'Oh my God,' the girl sobbed. 'She's dead.'

CHAPTER 3

A teenage boy wearing an Idlewood visor and a red change apron was kneeling outside the Tunnel of Love, pressing hard on the back of a dark-haired girl. The girl, dressed in pink, lay face-down on the grass near the entrance, her clothes soaked, her body motionless.

'Come on, breathe!' the boy pleaded. 'For God's sake, breathe!'

McKenzie found her way blocked by the crowd around the boy. 'What happened?' she asked.

'They just found her floating near the Tunnel's exit,' a woman answered. 'The boy who runs the ride pulled her out.'

Slowly, McKenzie pushed her way to the front of the crowd. The ticket taker and the girl were right beside the Tunnel's channel. For a brief moment McKenzie stared down at the water. A clump of snarled hair drifted past.

McKenzie tried to block it out, but she couldn't help remembering the sight of the girl's hair tangled in the paddle wheel. *Lilicat!*

'You're in the way!' the boy snapped at McKenzie. 'Come on,' he muttered to the girl again, 'please breathe!'

McKenzie felt her heart slow a little as she realized it *wasn't* Lilicat. The girl was younger than Lilicat, maybe fourteen or so. She was wearing a pink T-shirt and shorts, and she lay very still. McKenzie watched tensely. A dark bruise, almost like a handprint, covered the girl's ankle, and her skin was impossibly pale. Was she still alive?

The girl's chest suddenly heaved and she began to make choking sounds.

A second later a splash caught McKenzie's attention, and she looked up to see Lilicat standing in a swan-shaped boat that was just emerging from the Tunnel. A wave of relief washed over her, and she ran to the landing dock as Tony and Lilicat climbed from the boat.

'Hi, Mack, what's up?' asked Lilicat, who was clearly surprised to see her.

'Are you all right?' asked McKenzie, her voice rising with anxiety.

'We're fine,' Tony answered, his eyes on the girl who was lying on the ground. 'What's going on over there?'

'Didn't you see her in the water?' McKenzie asked. 'They just found her floating near the Tunnel exit.'

'We didn't see anything! Is she okay?' Lilicat looked shaken.

'I'd better check on her,' Tony said. 'Will you be all right for a few minutes?'

Lilicat nodded. McKenzie's eyes returned to the girl. 'I can't stand this, Lilicat,' she said. 'I have to see how she is.'

'Right,' Lilicat said, and the two girls made their way toward Tony.

'She's breathing,' reported the boy who'd pulled the girl from the water. He looked up at Tony. 'I think she'll be okay.'

'Has someone called Doc?'

'Yeah,' the boy answered, his attention back on the girl. 'I sent someone for the police, too.'

Tony knelt by the girl's side. 'What happened? Did she fall from one of the boats?'

The boy rattled the coins in his change apron nervously. 'I don't know, Tony. Honest, I never even saw her get on the ride. She must have sneaked in somehow.'

Tony frowned. 'That isn't easy. And falling

out of those boats isn't easy either – the sides are pretty high.'

'Maybe she was stoned or something,' the boy suggested.

'Maybe. But I think I'll go into the Tunnel and have a look.' Tony turned to Lilicat. 'Are you okay?'

'Sure.' She tried to smile.

McKenzie watched as Tony jogged to the Tunnel entrance and slipped through, walking on the narrow ledge that edged the channel.

'He's not gonna find anything in there,' the boy said to McKenzie and Lilicat. 'I say it's drugs.'

Just then the girl stirred. The fingers of her right hand moved. Her eyelids fluttered.

'No,' she said. Her voice was so soft that at first McKenzie wasn't sure she'd heard it. Then she spoke louder. 'No! Leave me alone!'

The boy hung back, but McKenzie crouched beside the girl. 'You're going to be fine,' she told her quietly. 'Just relax.'

The girl's blue eyes opened wide. 'Don't let him hurt me!' she screamed, bolting upright, her face distorted with fear.

'You're okay,' McKenzie said, holding the girl's shoulders. 'Nothing's going to hurt you.'

The girl started sobbing. 'He tried to kill me!'

'Who tried to kill you?'

The girl just shuddered and wept.

She was still sobbing when the doctor arrived, threading his way through the crowd of onlookers. McKenzie watched as he took the girl's pulse and blood pressure, shone a light into her eyes, and finally examined the bruise on her ankle. 'Can you tell me your name?' he asked.

Gradually, the girl's sobbing eased and she sat up. 'Andrea,' she said. 'Andrea Smith.'

'Is she all right?' Tony asked, emerging from the Tunnel.

'She'll be okay,' the doctor answered. 'But I want to take her into the hospital and run some tests – just to be sure.'

Tony ran a hand through his dark hair. 'I just wish this hadn't happened when my father was out of town.'

'Did you find anything in the Tunnel?' asked Lilicat.

'Nothing.'

'Out of my way. Out of my way, please.' Someone was elbowing through the crowd.

McKenzie turned and found herself standing next to a familiar stocky blond woman wearing a blue police uniform. Officer Rizzuto had been the one police officer who'd had enough faith in

McKenzie to let her help solve the Naugatuck baby-sitter murders a few months ago.

'McKenzie Gold,' said Officer Rizzuto, rubbing her pug nose. 'Are you in trouble again?' She smiled.

'Not this time,' said McKenzie. She introduced the police officer to Tony. Rizzuto listened as he explained what had happened, then said something to her male partner, who immediately vanished into the Tunnel of Love. Then Officer Rizzuto knelt by Andrea Smith and began to question her gently.

McKenzie couldn't hear what they were saying, but the police officer was taking notes and the girl seemed much calmer. So it surprised her when Andrea suddenly cried out, 'No! I'm telling you, someone pulled me!'

Lilicat nudged McKenzie, drawing her attention away from Andrea and the police officer. 'Look who's here.'

A tall, lanky teenage boy with shaggy blond hair walked down the midway, his eyes searching the crowd. 'Aidan!'

'Whoa!' Aidan grinned and stumbled backward as McKenzie threw herself into his arms, knocking the breath out of him. 'I'm glad to see you, too.' He bent to kiss her, then frowned at McKenzie's distracted response. 'Guess it's a good thing I came early. What's wrong?'

Trying to keep her voice calm, McKenzie told him about the near-drowning.

Aidan's eyes searched McKenzie's face. 'There's more, isn't there?'

McKenzie nodded. 'I was down at the other end of the midway, but I saw it happen, Aidan. I saw her hair tangled in the paddle wheel, and her pink shirt. I was terrified it was Lilicat.'

'Lilicat looks okay,' said Aidan. She was standing between Tony and Officer Rizzuto. 'Who's she with?'

'His name's Tony. His dad owns Idlewood. And he seems pretty nice, but some of the others who work here . . . .' McKenzie shuddered as she told him about Elijah and Madame Beaupree. 'I'm just glad we didn't get jobs here. I've had this weird feeling all day.'

'What kind of weird feeling?' Aidan asked, pulling her into his arms.

'Like there's a black cloud over this park . . . like there's something really bad here.'

'Hmmm,' Aidan said with a trace of doubt. 'Maybe I ought to take you home. I think a near-drowning is plenty of excitement for one day.'

'No.'

Aidan raised an eyebrow. 'No?'

'I need to talk to Officer Rizzuto,' said McKenzie. McKenzie watched as the doctor led Andrea away, then she saw Rizzuto's partner come out of the Tunnel. 'Let's see if the policeman found anything.'

Aidan followed McKenzie over to the Tunnel. There, Officer Rizzuto was talking with Tony. They were just in time to hear the other officer report, 'No luck. Couldn't find a thing.'

'Andrea wouldn't give me a home address,' said Officer Rizzuto. 'And she claims she has no family, all of which makes me suspicious of a last name like Smith. I think she's a runaway.'

'What would she be doing at Idlewood?' Tony asked.

'Hiding out, probably,' Officer Rizzuto replied. She flipped her pad closed. 'I'll be in touch soon,' she said to Tony.

'Wait!' McKenzie said. 'Could I see you for a minute? Alone?' She didn't mind talking in front of Lilicat and Aidan, but she didn't know Tony well enough to be talking about her special abilities in front of him.

'What is it, McKenzie?' asked the policewoman once they were a few feet away.

'I just wanted to tell you that I saw it all. I was at the other end of the park but I could see the girl drowning. As it happened.'

Officer Rizzuto's friendly expression didn't change. She knew McKenzie's powers could be trusted – they'd helped stop a serial killer only a few months before. 'I believe you,' she said. 'But, remember, she didn't drown.'

'She said someone pulled her. Do you know what she meant by that?'

Officer Rizzuto sighed. 'That's where it gets tricky. Andrea said someone pulled her from one of the boats, but the boy who works the ride never saw her get into a boat. Maybe he just missed seeing her. That's unlikely. I think she was inside the Tunnel all along, maybe hiding out on the ledge along the side, and fell in.'

'Why don't you believe what *she* says?' asked McKenzie.

'Because I think she's a runaway. And if she is, she won't tell anything near the truth because she doesn't want anyone to send her back home. Besides, the doctor thinks she may be on drugs.'

'You mean he thinks she was hallucinating?'

'It's possible. We'll find out from the blood tests.'

'What's going to happen to her?' Mack asked. She felt sorry for the girl.

'We'll check our photographs of missing kids. If Andrea's one of them, we'll get in touch with her family and find out why she was hiding out in an amusement park.'

'Her hair got caught in the boat's paddle wheel, didn't it?' McKenzie asked, once again seeing the vision that had sent her running toward the Tunnel of Love.

Officer Rizzuto's eyes narrowed. 'That's the one thing she told us that I didn't tell you. She's got a little bald patch where the wheel ripped her hair out. How did you know? Did you talk to her or did you – '

McKenzie nodded. 'I saw it.'

'All right, McKenzie.' The police officer took a deep breath. 'Tell me what *you* think happened.'

'I'm not sure,' McKenzie said unsteadily. What could she say that wouldn't sound ridiculous? That she felt some evil *something* hovering? 'I don't think Andrea was lying,' she said at last. 'There's that awful bruise on her ankle that looks sort of like the imprint of someone's fingers. Maybe someone did try to grab her and drown her.'

'Then again, maybe she was so drugged that

she stood up – either on the ledge or in one of the boats – and lost her balance,' said Officer Rizzuto. 'This isn't the first accident at Idlewood, you know. Amusement parks seem to bring out a wild streak in some people. Remember that story in the news last year about the girl who stood up in the roller coaster?'

Suddenly, McKenzie could barely hear Officer Rizzuto. It was eerie – she felt like someone's eyes were drilling into the back of her head. She looked over her shoulder. As far as she could tell, no one was watching her.

'These things happen,' the officer went on, as if making up her mind. 'Is something wrong?'

'No,' McKenzie said quickly. 'Just checking to see if my friends are still around. Anyway, what if Andrea *is* telling the truth? What'll you do next?'

The officer smiled. 'I appreciate your concern, McKenzie, but I think you should leave this one to us. Call us if you remember anything else, though.'

'Of course,' McKenzie assured her. But she didn't really want to get involved. The eerie feeling Idlewood Park gave her made her want to get away from the place. And stay away.

She went back to her friends, feeling those eyes on her the whole time. She tried to put the strange feeling out of her mind. Have a good time with your friends, Mack, she told herself. Like a normal person.

'Great first date, huh?' Tony was joking to Lilicat as McKenzie rejoined them. McKenzie thought he looked embarrassed by all the trouble – in a way he was their host, after all. But he wasn't too embarrassed to reach over, squeeze Lilicat's hand, and hold on to it.

Aidan, who was standing to the side, winked at McKenzie.

McKenzie couldn't help grinning.

'Stop that, you two!' Lilicat said, trying to look indignant.

Tony smiled. 'I hope this accident won't scare you away for good,' he said to Aidan and McKenzie. 'Usually Idlewood is a blast. I've lived here for years, and I haven't gotten bored with it yet.' He reached into his pocket, took out three free day-long passes and handed one to each of them. 'Give us another try. I promise you'll have more fun next time.' Then he took a deep breath. 'So, are we on for next Saturday night, Lilith?'

Lilicat smiled. 'I can't wait.'

'Lilith?' McKenzie mouthed to Aidan. Hardly anyone called Lilicat by her real name.

Aidan raised his eyebrows comically high and shrugged.

As she walked to the parking lot with her friends, McKenzie tried to ignore the feeling that someone was watching her. It was like trying to ignore a spider crawling up her back.

CHAPTER 4

The Fat Lady entered the stuffy canvas tent and gave the woman in the red velvet turban a contemptuous glance. 'Get out of my way, you stupid fake.' Pushing Madame Beaupree aside, she sat down in front of the crystal ball. The chair shuddered beneath her weight.

The elastic of her custom-made white lace-bottomed leggings cut into her waist, reminding her of how much she hated the baby-doll image Mr. Robards insisted on. She hated the pink pinafore and the patent leather shoes with their dainty straps. She loathed pulling her thinning red hair into two skimpy pigtails. But the old man claimed people would find the whole thing funny – a fat lady who looked like a little girl. It wasn't funny to her. Far from it.

'Dinah, you don't understand,' Madame Beaupree said. 'That girl – the one with the long red hair – looked into the crystal ball and saw the runaway.' She finished lamely. 'Even before I did.'

'What a surprise,' Dinah muttered. 'You couldn't read the future if it was printed in the newspaper.'

Madame Beaupree drew herself up indignantly. 'It's not every day someone comes in who can see – '

'Lots of people have the Sight,' Dinah said flatly. 'Most of 'em don't have enough of it to see past their noses, but sooner or later someone was bound to show up who did. The question is – just how much did the girl see?'

Dinah leaned her elbows on the rickety table. She closed her eyes and rubbed her hands over the ball, humming something tuneless. Then she hunched over the crystal ball, green eyes wide. She'd find out who this girl was that Madame Beaupree claimed was psychic.

First she called up the girl's image. Silently she studied her wide-set gray-green eyes, the freckles across her nose, the determined but generous mouth. A name came to her, an unusual one. 'McKenzie Gold,' she whispered softly. 'And just where are you right now, Miss Gold?' She saw the auburn-haired girl in the park. She was sitting on a bench, talking with a policewoman. Then she was walking with her friends, walking along and laughing. Dinah knew immediately that the old phony Beaupree was right for once. The girl had the Sight. Even now the girl glanced around her, as if she felt Dinah watching.

Dinah leaned closer to the ball, fighting an unexpected surge of jealousy. The girl could have been her, years ago. Once Dinah had been young and slender, had had long, auburn hair. Now her body was a joke that people paid to laugh at. All she really had left was the Sight. But this girl had the Sight, and everything else, too. And if Dinah's hunch was right, the girl's Sight was nearly as strong as her own.

Madame Beaupree squinted into the crystal ball. 'What's she doing now?'

'She's leaving, but she'll be back. I can feel it.'

Madame Beaupree plucked at her caftan sleeve. 'She seemed like a nice girl.'

Dinah ignored the fortune-teller and let herself be drawn into the world of the crystal ball, a world where past, present, and future tangled like satin ribbons. She sought the future. And she found it.

The park. Still. Still as death. Carousel horses

strewn across the midway. The Hall of Mirrors a pile of broken shards. The Catacombs boarded up . . . if the girl with the auburn hair was allowed to interfere.

'No,' Dinah said. 'I won't let that happen.' Without Idlewood, where would they go? There was no place else for them to live. She had to protect this place, keep its secrets. No matter what happened.

She slipped deeper, looking toward the future. A thin line of sweat beaded her upper lip as she sorted through the events to come. There were ways to change what would be. She pushed at the future with her mind until she felt something give.

The images in the crystal ball darkened and rearranged themselves.

The auburn-haired girl was running through the twisting passageways of the Catacombs, terrified and alone. Panicked, she went deeper into the tunnels until at last she entered the alcove that was never meant to be entered, the alcove where He lived. The vision ended abruptly. Nothing more was to be seen in the crystal. Nothing more was necessary.

Dinah's lips curled into a smile. 'Yes,' she said, 'that's more like it. We're going to solve two problems at once.' She looked up and fixed her eyes on Madame Beaupree. 'Tell everyone we meet tonight.'

That night after the park closed down, a strange crowd gathered by candlelight in Madame Beaupree's tent. Shorty and Stretchman sat side by side in the tent's darkest corner. Across from them stood Elijah, talking to the Fire Eater. The Strong Man guarded the entrance, arms crossed and legs spread.

Madame Beaupree set her chair beside Shorty and Stretchman. 'She's in a terrible mood,' she whispered to them. 'Even worse than usual.'

Stretchman looked very nervous and actually seemed to shrink a little. Only Shorty struck a defiant pose, hands on hips, chest out – ready for anything. 'She doesn't scare me,' he rasped.

Footsteps crunched on the gravel just outside the tent, and everyone inside shifted nervously. The tent's canvas flap parted and a tall, platinum-blonde, barefoot woman wearing a gold lamé bikini entered, a thick python draped around her neck. 'We're the last ones here, darling,' she cooed to the snake. She never spoke to anyone else. 'It's all your fault, snookums – you and your finicky appetite.' She stroked the snake as she made her way across the tent.

'One of these days she's going to wind up in

the loony bin,' Madame Beaupree whispered to Shorty.

'Did you hear what she said about us, darling?' the Snake Woman said to her python. 'That nasty old fake doesn't like us very much. But don't let her upset you, sweet thing. None of her predictions ever come true.'

Madame Beaupree muttered something under her breath, and Shorty snickered.

No one heard her coming, but suddenly the Fat Lady stood in the entrance, holding the tent flap high. Her bulk blocked most of the glare from the security lights outside.

She stepped in and dropped the tent flap, then made her way to the thronelike chair she used for the sideshow. It was a dark, heavy piece of furniture carved with anguished faces that grimaced just above her shoulders. 'I hold every one of you responsible for that runaway getting away today,' she said angrily.

'It wasn't our fault – ' Shorty began.

Dinah silenced him with a glare. 'I've just come from talking with Him. He's hungry, really hungry this time.' She turned on Elijah. 'You let that girl get away.'

Elijah's eyes were wide. 'I – I had her by the ankle,' he stammered, 'but her hair got caught in the paddle and another boat was coming through. I knew Tony was in the Tunnel – I didn't want to risk being seen. So I had to – '

'Silence!' Dinah thundered. She heaved herself from the chair, stalked across the crowded tent, and thrust her face into Stretch's. 'Elijah's not the only one who ruined everything – Stretch. *You* pointed that snoopy red-haired girl right at the Tunnel of Love. How could you do such a stupid thing!'

'I – I'm sorry,' Stretchman stuttered.

'You're cowards, all of you,' Dinah told them. 'Why do I work so hard to keep Him happy? I should just let Him loose on the lot of you! It's no worse than you deserve!'

The silence in the tent intensified. The freaks knew Dinah was capable of anything.

She turned and approached the Snake Woman, who seemed to be paying more attention to the python than to what Dinah was saying. 'Do you think you're safe from Him?' she demanded. 'Do you think this is a game? He'll eat you and make you His and then come back for more. He doesn't care if we're freaks or norms.

'In fact,' she went on, turning to peer nastily at Shorty, 'He might prefer those of us who can't run very fast.'

Shorty swallowed hard, his eyes wide, and

he seemed to deflate. His false courage of a few minutes ago was gone.

Slowly Dinah settled herself into her chair again and sighed. 'He's still not satisfied, and He won't be satisfied until we find Him another girl. Unless, of course, any of you would like to volunteer . . . Snake Woman?'

Snake Woman stiffened but said nothing. The python coiled tighter around her and she patted it protectively.

Dinah said, 'He wants a girl. The red-headed girl is a snoop and dangerous – I saw her talking to the police this afternoon. So we're going to solve two problems at once. The next time she comes nosing around the park, grab her.'

Elijah bravely stepped in front of Dinah's chair. 'Killing the red-haired girl will only make things worse.'

'Oh?' Dinah said with mock sweetness. 'Pray tell me why, Elijah.'

'She came to the park with friends. She knows Tony, too. She's not a runaway. If anything happened to her, the park would be crawling with police, and that's the last thing we need.'

'What do you suggest we do, then?' Dinah barked. 'Throw one of our own to the Evil?'

Shorty shifted nervously, and Dinah licked her lips. 'He needs live victims, you know.'

Elijah refused to back down. 'Find people like the runaway – people with no ties. It's the only way. We can't afford an investigation.'

Dinah was silent for a moment, wondering how much to tell them. She wasn't about to let the others know the girl had the Sight, and fortunately, Madame Beaupree was too afraid of her to squeal. The less they knew about that, the better. 'If we let her live, it will be worse,' she said at last. 'I used the crystal today. Do you know what I saw? Idlewood closed, every-thing in ruins. The red-haired girl is a meddler. If we let her live, she's going to bring us all down. She'll destroy everything we have.'

The freaks looked at one another miserably. They couldn't let Idlewood close. There weren't many other amusement parks like it left in the world – and without a freak show to work in they all would be lost.

'Not if we can scare her off,' said Elijah. 'If she comes back, we'll scare her so badly that she'll never come near here again.'

'And if that doesn't work?'

The Tattooed Man shrugged his big shoulders, and the patterns on his chest and arms rippled. 'Then we get rid of her.' He hesitated. 'If we can't scare her off, then we give her to Him.'

Dinah nodded. 'Fine, Elijah.' The chair groaned beneath her as she leaned forward. 'I know McKenzie Gold will be back – and she won't scare easily.'

CHAPTER 5

A **rough pink** tongue licked her nose, and McKenzie rolled over in bed, trying to ignore the cat and finish the dream that had just begun. The cat licked her again. 'All right already, Blue,' she mumbled. 'I'll get up.' She sat up, squinting at the bright summer sunlight that poured through her bedroom window.

She ran a hand through the cat's thick black fur. 'Don't you know it's summer vacation?' she asked him. 'I'm supposed to sleep late.' Blue purred happily and butted her with his head. McKenzie looked at her alarm clock. The cat was right. It was almost ten in the morning; she ought to be awake. And yet she wished she'd finished the dream. It had something to do with Idlewood, she was sure of it.

Belting her robe over the faded red T-shirt

she always slept in, McKenzie went downstairs. Her mother was standing in front of the living room mirror, combing a flyaway strand of hair. Like McKenzie's, it was auburn.

When she saw her daughter reflected in the mirror, Mrs. Gold smiled. 'Morning, Sleepyhead,' she said. 'I have an early appointment, but I'll be back by one o'clock.'

McKenzie ran a hand through her own hair. 'Sure, Mom. Is Dad at work already?'

'Yes. Mabel called in sick with bursitis.'

'I could go over and give him a hand.' Mr. Gold ran the hardware store that his grandfather had started. McKenzie often helped out when he was short-staffed. Working in a hardware store wasn't exactly thrilling, but she enjoyed spending time with her father.

'I know he'd appreciate it, but I need you to keep an eye on Jimmy. He's riding his bike out front.' Mrs. Gold slung her purse over her shoulder. 'I'll see you later, dear.'

The phone rang at eleven o'clock that morning.

Jimmy was in the kitchen, raiding the refrigerator. He bolted for the phone, leaving the refrigerator door wide open. 'Mack, it's for you!'

McKenzie picked up the phone, wondering who it could be. It definitely wasn't Aidan. If it was, Jimmy would be making kissing noises and crooning, 'Lover boy.'

'Miss Gold?' a cheery voice asked.

'Yes.'

'Philip Berrian of the Total Tomato. You filled out a summer job application?'

'Yes,' McKenzie said, trying to remember which mall the restaurant was in. 'Last week.'

'I was very impressed with you, Miss Gold. You seemed like a Total Tomato type of person. Are you still interested in the job?'

'Definitely,' McKenzie said, wondering only briefly what type of person a Total Tomato type was. Mostly, she was relieved. It was nice to sleep in once in a while, but she was going to need money for college.

'Can you start today at three?'

'Sure, I'll be glad to.' Mr. Berrian sounded friendly and nice. McKenzie thought she'd probably like working for him.

'Great! I'll see you then.'

'Yes, sir.'

Two seconds later McKenzie called Lilicat. 'Guess what?' she said as soon as she heard her friend's voice. 'Mr. Berrian called from the Total Tomato and I've got a job!'

Lilicat laughed. 'I was just going to call you with the same news. Did he tell you that you were the Total Tomato type?'

'You mean I'm not unique?' McKenzie asked in mock alarm.

'I never thought of myself as particularly tomatolike either,' Lilicat confessed. Her voice became wistful. 'I still wish we could have gotten jobs at Idlewood.'

'If we worked at the park, you'd never get anything done, you'd be so busy staring at Tony.'

'That's my kind of job, all right.'

'Do you want me to pick you up?' McKenzie asked, ignoring Jimmy who was standing in front of her, clutching his stomach in a terrible imitation of someone starving to death.

'Sure. At two-thirty?'

'I'll see you then,' McKenzie said. 'Jimmy's bugging me for lunch already. I'd better just make it for him.'

At ten minutes of three McKenzie and Lilicat walked into the Total Tomato, a small franchise at the Lakeville Mall that specialized in dishes like tomato soup, tomato casserole, stuffed tomatoes, and tomato salads.

Mr. Berrian strode up to the girls and shook

their hands. With his round red face, he looked a little like a tomato himself. 'Yes,' he said, examining the girls briefly. 'You'll fit right in. Come with me.'

They walked through a swinging metal door into the kitchen. Mr. Berrian pointed to a pretty dark-haired girl who was chopping vegetables. 'That's Kirsten. She's cooking today.'

'She isn't the regular cook?' Lilicat asked.

'We don't have a regular cook,' Mr. Berrian explained. 'Everyone here does everything. We rotate jobs.'

Suddenly McKenzie had a feeling that the Total Tomato was going to be an experience she wouldn't forget.

'You do know tomatoes, don't you?' asked Mr. Berrian earnestly.

'We'll learn,' McKenzie promised.

He nodded approvingly. 'That's the Total Tomato attitude.' He continued their tour of the kitchen, briefly explaining the uses of the various machines. Finally he said, 'I've been so anxious to get you started I forgot to let you change. Your uniforms are in the rest room, back that way.' He gave them a big smile. 'Why don't you two change, and then we'll start you on the Total Tomato Training Track.'

In the rest room McKenzie put on a pair of

red stretch pants and a matching top that looked about her size. Lilicat had to roll her pants up at the bottom.

They rejoined Mr. Berrian in the kitchen.

'Let's get to work, girls,' he said, rubbing his hands together briskly. 'Ah!' He shook his index finger. 'Can't forget your caps.'

He reached into a deep metal drawer and pulled out two things that looked as if someone had gone crazy with scissors on a piece of red and green felt.

McKenzie took hers. The caps were made to look like the top of a tomato, complete with stem and five pointy pieces dangling in various directions. She sneaked a peek at Lilicat, who was staring at her cap as if it would bite.

Mr. Berrian clapped his hands together cheerfully and said, 'Let's go, girls! I want to get you started behind the counter.'

McKenzie and Lilicat plunked their caps on their heads and followed him out of the kitchen.

It seemed like hours later that Mr. Berrian was convinced they could handle the counter and left them on their own. Lilicat immediately yanked the cap from her head. 'I can't let Tony see me in this.'

'So don't tell him you work here.'

'I called him right after I talked to you.'

'What did he say?'

'We couldn't really talk. He was showing someone how to operate a ride. He said he'd call tonight to find out how my first day went.' Lilicat stuck the cap back on her head. 'Maybe I'll tell him I didn't take the job after all.'

'Oh, come on. It can't be that bad.' McKenzie glanced at the stainless steel refrigerator that was almost as good as a mirror. Yes, it could be that bad.

'Think Aidan will like it?' Lilicat teased.

McKenzie groaned. 'He'll love it – he'll never let me live it down.'

'At least we're in this together.'

The girls laughed as Mr. Berrian rejoined them. 'That's what I like to see,' he said. 'Good cheer.' He introduced them to Kirsten, the girl they'd be working with most often. She seemed nice enough but not overly friendly. Kirsten left her working post to wait on the few customers while Mr. Berrian showed the girls how to prepare various dishes.

He pulled a tomato topped with bubbling mozzarella out of the oven. 'Did you know that a plain four-ounce tomato contains only twenty-five calories? There's nothing like a fat-free treat!'

It actually looked pretty good, McKenzie thought. Sort of like a pizza without the crust.

The girls worked in the kitchen and behind the counter all afternoon. Mr. Berrian was cheerful and patient, although he told them more than they'd ever wanted to know about his favorite vegetable. Fruit, actually. One of the first things he made clear was that a tomato was really a fruit. McKenzie shook her head as she cut up another fruit; it was going to be a weird summer.

At eight that evening, when their shift was officially over, McKenzie and Lilicat turned in their uniforms and started out the door. 'Remember,' Mr. Berrian called out, 'a cup of tomato juice has zero cholesterol!'

Lilicat said, 'If he doesn't cut the tomato trivia, I may strangle him before the summer ends.'

'Hey, at least you get to wait on tables tomorrow,' McKenzie pointed out. 'I'll be in the kitchen with him.'

By the time she reported for work on Thursday, McKenzie felt totally confused. To encourage 'an atmosphere of helping and sharing,' Total Tomato employees switched jobs from one day to the next. McKenzie had done food prep on Tuesday and waited on tables Wed-

51

nesday. By Thursday she figured she'd probably forgotten half of what she'd learned how to do in the kitchen.

Mr. Berrian had taken the day off. That was one good thing, McKenzie thought as she put tomatoes into the blender.

She watched as the blender began to spin. Around and around.

The kitchen faded away and in its place appeared the carousel at Idlewood. Only there was something wrong.

The carousel spun silently and slowly, as if it couldn't get enough power to move at the right speed.

A teenage girl with short black hair rode by, draped over a painted wooden horse, her head lolling at an impossible angle. Dead.

Another girl rode by, clutching one of the horses that rose and fell, rose and fell in silence. Her skin was a bluish gray and her blue skirt dripped muddy water onto the wooden floor of the carousel. The girl stared straight ahead, her eyes flat and still.

A girl in a yellow summer dress, white gloves, and a white hat rode by next. Her body was slumped in a chariot seat, her mouth open in a silent scream of terror. Blood dripped from her throat.

The black-haired girl with the broken neck rode by again. McKenzie noticed that she was dressed in bell-bottom jeans and a peasant blouse, like someone from the sixties.

McKenzie became aware of a voice singing. Getting louder. An old song.

'*Someone's in the kitchen with Dinah,*
Someone's in the kitchen, I know . . .'

The carousel slowed and stopped, but the voice kept singing. Someone lurched across the wooden floor of the carousel, bumping from horse to horse.

A hand grabbed the silver pole of a horse frozen in mid-prance. A hand that was slowly rotting to the bone.

The thing that had once been a man stared at McKenzie with one eye. The other eye hung halfway from its socket.

'Want a ride, McKenzie?'

McKenzie screamed as the man tore his heart from his chest, and held it out to her.

CHAPTER 6

A hand shook her shoulder. 'Mack! Mack, snap out of it! What's wrong with you?'

McKenzie slumped in relief.

'Are you okay? Did you cut yourself?' Lilicat grabbed McKenzie's fingers and ran them under a faucet. 'Thank God it's only pureed tomatoes!' she said. 'For a minute there, I thought you had blood all over your hands.'

McKenzie took a deep breath. 'I guess I . . . I was seeing things.'

'It looked like you were hypnotized by the blender.'

Was I? McKenzie wondered. She looked around and realized she must have taken the lid off the blender when she was working, because pureed tomatoes dripped from everything in the kitchen. 'We'd better clean up before Kirsten sees this.' McKenzie grabbed a rag and began wiping, her heart still thudding.

As they cleaned, McKenzie told Lilicat about her vision, though she kept most of the gorier details to herself.

'You were singing "Someone's in the kitchen with Dinah," ' Lilicat said. 'I could hear you all the way out in the dining room.'

'*I* was singing it?' McKenzie asked. 'That was me?'

'There wasn't anyone else in the kitchen.'

'I guess not,' McKenzie said slowly. 'But in the vision someone else sang it.' She shivered as she remembered the mutilated man. 'I don't know who he was.'

Lilicat shrugged. 'That's so weird.' She put a comforting hand on McKenzie's shoulder. 'You know what I think?'

'What?'

'That working in "tomato heaven" here has gone to your brain.'

'You're probably right,' McKenzie agreed, but the song kept running through her mind, as if it were the key to a secret door. McKenzie shuddered, wondering what lay behind that door. Later that night McKenzie was relaxing in her window seat with Blue and her tattered copy of *Green Mansions* when her father called up the stairs, 'Mack, phone.'

McKenzie got downstairs in time to hear her father saying, 'Tomato tedium? That's a good one, Lilicat.' He handed the phone to McKenzie with a grin.

'Mack,' Lilicat said, 'are you feeling okay?'

'Fine.' Actually she felt better this evening than she had in days. When she'd sat down with her book, she'd forgotten all about the Total Tomato, Idlewood Park, and everything else.

'Well, I'm not. I can't wait 'til Saturday night to see Tony. He's going back to college in September, you know. How about coming to the park with me tomorrow?' Lilicat sounded eager, but McKenzie wasn't crazy about the idea. She hesitated.

'Mack, are you there?'

You can't keep running away from things, McKenzie told herself. The visions won't go away. Sooner or later, you'll have to deal with whatever is going on there. 'Sure, I'll go,' she said as casually as she could. 'Mind if I ask Aidan?'

' 'Course not.'

'He's working until nine tonight. How about

if I call you back tomorrow morning and let you know what time?'

'Great,' Lilicat said. 'I can't wait to see Tony again.'

McKenzie called Aidan around nine-thirty.

'How's my little tomato today?' he asked in his best Mr. Berrian imitation.

'Very funny.' Aidan had stopped in at the restaurant on Wednesday. He'd doubled over laughing when he first saw McKenzie, and then complimented Mr. Berrian on the uniforms while McKenzie glared at him.

'I like that boy,' Mr. Berrian had said as Aidan left. 'Do you think he'd be interested in a job?'

'Doubtful,' McKenzie had answered, trying not to laugh. 'He's already working at a camera store and filling in for vacationing photographers on the town paper. Plus he's got a part-time job at the Gap.'

'So what's new in the tomato biz?' Aidan was asking cheerfully.

'Not much.' McKenzie decided not to tell him about her vision. Aidan would probably advise her not to go back to the park, and while she'd love to listen to him, she knew she couldn't. 'Lilicat and I are going to Idlewood tomorrow to use our free passes. She can't get through another day without seeing Tony.

57

And,' she added softly, 'it seems like ages since I've seen you. The tomato visit doesn't count.'

'Will you wear your uniform?' he teased.

'Aidan!'

'Well, geez, you looked so cute and – '

McKenzie took a deep breath, thinking she'd like to punch him on his 'cute' nose. 'Do you want to go to Idlewood tomorrow or not?' she asked patiently.

'Of course I do,' he told her. 'Maybe I'll even get you on the roller coaster.'

'Don't bet on it.'

'This place is packed,' McKenzie noted as she, Lilicat, and Aidan entered Idlewood on Friday afternoon. 'You'd never guess a girl almost drowned here less than a week ago.'

'Well, she's okay, isn't she?' Lilicat asked. 'The story in the paper said she'd be fine.'

McKenzie frowned. The three-inch column the newspaper had given to Andrea Smith's story had said very little – only that she had fallen off a boat in the Tunnel of Love and almost drowned. Nothing had been written about her terror and confusion, or the fact that she was a runaway.

Tony met them at the gate. He was wearing jeans, cowboy boots, and a T-shirt that proclaimed, 'I survived the Catacombs – *this* time.' McKenzie watched his eyes light on Lilicat. The two of them looked as if they were dying to fling themselves into each other's arms for some kind of endless Hollywood kiss.

McKenzie squeezed Aidan's hand. She was glad he was here today.

Lilicat was the first to look away. 'Uh – do you think the lines for the Catacombs are long today?' she asked Tony. 'I can't wait to see what it's like.'

'You'll *love* it,' Tony said. 'I can get you on the list so you don't have to wait in line. I wish I could go in with you, but I've got work to do.'

Lilicat pouted. 'I think you work too hard.'

'Are you kidding? This is an amusement park! It's fun! Anyway, I'll meet you later.' Tony led the way to the Catacombs. 'You've never seen anything like the Catacombs, I promise you that,' he said proudly. 'You go in groups of four or less,' he added. 'Groups enter every seven minutes.'

He talked with the girl who sat in a little wooden booth taking tickets, then came back. 'You can go in about four o'clock. I'll meet you out here around quarter after and I'll be able to take my supper break with you.' He hesitated, then kissed Lilicat on the cheek.

She beamed.

'See you at four-fifteen.' Tony strolled off down the midway.

'What'll we do till four?' Lilicat asked, her eyes still on Tony.

Aidan kept a straight face as he said, 'Mack wants to ride the Cougar.'

'You're kidding!' An astonished Lilicat turned to McKenzie. 'You hate roller coasters.'

'He's kidding, all right.' McKenzie threw a light punch at Aidan's arm.

'You won't go on, even for me?' he teased.

'Forget it.' McKenzie put her arm around Aidan's waist, and they started back up the midway.

'How about the Whip, then?'

McKenzie rolled her eyes. 'Look!' she said, determined to change the subject. 'Isn't that Lumpy Johnson and his sister over there?'

Lumpy was the sports editor on the school paper, and neither McKenzie nor Aidan really liked him, but McKenzie insisted on dragging Aidan and Lilicat over to say hello. They spent a few minutes catching up on everyone's summer. Then they spent an hour in the Fun House and on some of the tamer rides.

A few minutes before four, McKenzie, Aidan, and Lilicat headed for the Catacombs. As they waited their turn, Lilicat read the sign at the entrance aloud:

1. *This is not a ride for wimps or people who mind a little dirt on their shoes.*
2. *You walk . . . or run . . . the entire route.*
3. *Once inside you'll have to make some choices. What happens to you depends on the choices you make.*
4. *There are no right answers.*
5. *Keep your eyes and ears open. Look for the hidden crevices and secret passages. You may need them.*
6. *Bring back a gold coin and get a free 'I survived the Catacombs' T-shirt.*

'Sounds pretty scary,' Aidan said, giving McKenzie a meaningful glance. 'Could be even worse than the roller coaster.'

'Oh, shut up,' McKenzie murmured. She knew Aidan was only kidding, but she didn't want to admit he might be right.

The door to the Catacombs looked like an old mine shaft, complete with weathered wooden beams. A breeze brushed across the entrance, carrying with it the dank smell of wet dirt and rock. A thought prickled in McKenzie's mind: *Don't go in there.*

Groups emerged from the Catacombs laughing and talking about what they'd seen inside. *Don't go in there.* Her heart beat slow and hard. But she couldn't listen to her own fear. She had to go in.

Finally the ticket-taker signaled that it was their turn. They walked beneath the thick door-way, and the smell of dirt and rock became stronger. It was quiet inside except for the sound of water trickling down the walls. And it was dark but for a faint phosphorescent glow from the rock walls.

The tunnel descended straight and slow for a few hundred yards. Then it forked. The left side curved away on the level; the right side led downward. The right side was darker.

'I think I hear the group before us down that way.' Aidan pointed left. 'Let's go to the right.'

'Okay,' McKenzie said, trying to control her rising sense of panic. They walked three abreast on the sandy floor until the tunnel narrowed. Then Aidan led the way and McKenzie brought up the rear.

The narrowness of the passage with its solid rock walls seemed threatening somehow. It's just a ride in an amusement park, McKenzie told herself. We'll be out of here in a few minutes, back in the sunlight again.

No one spoke. The only sounds were the occasional tinkle of water sliding down the walls into a small pool, and the sounds of their own footsteps.

Even Aidan looked relieved when the passage widened a little and they could walk side by side. McKenzie took his hand and leaned close. That felt much better.

They turned a corner. On their left the passage opened into a grotto. A pile of gold coins sparkled at the bottom of the pool at its center.

'Anybody for a T-shirt?' Aidan asked. They entered the grotto. Aidan was reaching for the coins when a piece of the wall slid open as quietly as a well-oiled door, and two Lizard Men leaped through the opening. They held guns that looked like something out of a science fiction movie, and aimed them at the three friends.

McKenzie, Lilicat, and Aidan backed up slowly.

'You cannot escape,' one of the creatures said in a synthesized voice. His yellow eyes flickered in the half-light of the cave.

McKenzie, Aidan, and Lilicat turned to run,

but an iron gate dropped from a hidden crevice and clanged shut.

'We're trapped!' cried Lilicat.

CHAPTER 7

McKenzie began to search the walls of the grotto for a secret passageway, for anything that would lead them out of the Catacombs. She pulled on pieces of rock that seemed loose. She pressed against the wall. Nothing. Beside her, Aidan and Lilicat were doing the same, Aidan muttering, 'There's got to be a way out.'

The Lizard Men advanced, hissing. McKenzie turned around just long enough to see that their tongues flitted in and out like those of snakes.

'I found something!' Lilicat said. She'd lifted a small outcropping of rock that turned out to be hollow. Underneath was a lever cleverly made to look like a piece of rock.

'Pull it!' Aidan yelled. He jumped in front of the girls, shielding them from the Lizard Men. Suddenly he dropped out of sight.

'Aidan!' McKenzie screamed. Then she was falling, too.

They slid down a padded chute, one after the other.

Aidan whooped as he landed on the thick foam mat at the bottom. McKenzie slid into him and Lilicat crashed into her.

McKenzie stood up and dusted herself off, a little shaken but laughing.

'Definitely not your average ride,' Aidan said. McKenzie couldn't see him at all; she could only hear his voice in the darkness. Total darkness.

'Let's feel around for a way out of here,' McKenzie said.

They began to shuffle around, feeling the rocky walls, but no one got very far. The room was small.

'It smells like a zoo in here.'

'Sshh,' Aidan said. 'Something's moving.'

All three froze.

Something shifted in the corner farthest from them. Something big, by the sound of it.

'It's breathing,' Lilicat whispered, stepping back closer to the others.

The thing sniffed, as if hunting them by their scent.

McKenzie's eyes had begun to adjust to the

light. A hairy shape was shuffling their way. 'Let's get out of here,' she said. All her determination to be brave was gone. She spotted an archway into the passage outside. If only they could get past the creature.

'Run!' Aidan said.

The creature snuffled at their legs and growled as they ran past, but no one stopped to see if it followed them out the door.

They found themselves in a low, winding passage, Lilicat first, Aidan behind her, McKenzie last.

'We'll have to crawl, I guess.' Lilicat dropped to her hands and knees.

The darkness was again complete and McKenzie could hardly even see Aidan in front of her, let alone see beyond him to Lilicat. Her friend's voice sounded tiny and far away.

It's like another world down here, McKenzie thought. The world of the Catacombs. She shivered and wiped some slimy mud from her hands. It's just a ride, she told herself for the fiftieth time. Still, she couldn't wait to get out.

She realized she'd fallen behind when she couldn't see or hear anyone in front of her anymore.

'Aidan?' her voice bounced up the passage with a hollow sound.

'Mack! Up this way.'

Her heart began to beat again. He was probably straight ahead. Was it her imagination, or was it getting darker and darker?

The passage curved sharply to the right. She heard a sound up ahead. 'Wait up, guys!' she called. The rock walls were rubbing her arms on both sides now. It couldn't get much narrower.

Stop panicking, she told herself. It's all in fun.

Now the air felt cooler. McKenzie reached above her head. No wonder. The ceiling was higher here. She stood slowly, letting her muscles adjust to walking upright again.

But when she took a step forward, her knee hit solid rock. She put her hand out in front of her. More solid rock. She'd hit a dead end.

McKenzie gulped hard. This wasn't possible. She'd been following Aidan and Lilicat. Where were they? Had they taken another turn? Were they somehow on the other side of this wall? 'Aidan? Lilicat?' she called out. 'Where are you?'

There was no answer.

She turned back to retrace her steps, crawling as the passage became lower, stopping every few inches to feel for the turn she'd missed.

And then she realized that finding Aidan and Lilicat was the least of her problems. Someone had found *her*.

She heard a faint rustling, like cloth against rock, and then what could only be footsteps. It wasn't Aidan or Lilicat. She'd grown so used to the sound of their footsteps in the passageways that she knew someone else was in the darkness with her. These steps were much slower and heavier. They belonged to someone who was much bigger than she was.

'McKenzie.' The deep voice echoed through the silent corridor. 'McKenzie.'

McKenzie leaned against the rocky surface, not daring to breathe. She fought down her own panic, trying to make her mind work. The passage widened in front of her. Where was the voice coming from? Above her? Behind?

'Lost, little girl?'

She felt the skin on the back of her neck crawl. Whoever it was and wherever he was, he was no friend.

'Come on, McKenzie.' The footsteps stopped but the deep voice was closer. Much closer. She could almost feel his breath. 'Let me show you the way. You could be down here a long, long time. A pretty little girl like you don't want to spend her life in the darkness.'

McKenzie bit down on her knuckles so she wouldn't scream.

She heard the footsteps again. They were coming from the right. She was sure of it. Moving as quietly as she could, she edged to the left.

Something beind her made a creaking sound, like a crypt being opened. McKenzie turned and froze, her eyes wide. A hidden door in the rock wall was sliding open.

She was too terrified to be surprised. She tried to calm herself enough to use her special sense. What was she looking at – a trap or the way out?

'McKenzie, I've been waiting for you.' He was right behind her, getting closer with every second. Without another thought, McKenzie ran into the open room.

She shut her eyes for a second against an unexpected glare. This room was lighter. Torches flared from the walls. The place looked like a rough-hewn chapel. In front of her was an altar made from a flat rock laid across two other rocks. McKenzie approached the altar, drawn by a feeling she couldn't resist.

A wind swept through the room, dimming the torches. A moment later they flared again, and McKenzie saw a girl with long, straight auburn hair. The girl wore jeans and a T-shirt. Her back was turned to McKenzie. Slowly, the girl walked towards the altar. She stood in front of it, perfectly motionless. Then she knelt. She bowed her head, her long hair gleaming in the torchlight. Who is she? McKenzie wondered. What am I seeing?

The girl's body suddenly jerked forward and her hands flew to her throat, pulling at something McKenzie couldn't see. She was struggling, trying to get away from whatever held her.

McKenzie stared, unable to move. The girl was being strangled!

Never making a sound, the girl continued to fight. She wrenched herself around, turning to face McKenzie, silently begging for help.

But McKenzie couldn't help her. Instead she gave in to the terror and screamed. The girl was McKenzie herself.

CHAPTER 8

McKenzie's own screams rang in her ears as she watched the vision of herself being strangled.

'Go ahead, scream,' the deep voice told her. 'No one will hear you.'

Still screaming, she turned to run, but the door she'd come through had closed. She beat against it, but the door wouldn't give.

Gasping, she spun around and searched for another way out. She felt as if she couldn't get enough air.

She pushed against the wall and suddenly a door swung open. McKenzie ran through it.

She stopped short. Two or three yards outside the room, the Catacombs floor opened onto a sheer drop-off, so deep she couldn't see the bottom. McKenzie's stomach twisted into a knot.

A rope bridge swayed back and forth across the chasm. She could just barely make out the other side in the gloom.

Then her old fear of heights hit. Hard. So hard that she doubled over with nausea. She knew she'd have to cross the bridge, and at the same time she felt sure she'd never make it. She straightened up, still clutching her stomach with both arms, and stepped toward the bridge. It looked to her like little more than a fragile row of matchsticks, but she kept her eyes on it nevertheless, to avoid seeing the yawning spaces on either side of it.

She gripped both sides of the rope and stepped on it. The bridge dropped a foot under her weight. Don't look down! she told herself and took a few steps. The bridge swayed from side to side, and her stomach swayed with it.

One foot at a time, she began to inch her way across the bridge.

'Mack! Are you all right?' Aidan stood just on the other side of the bridge. Lilicat was behind him, holding up her hands in a victory signal. They both knew McKenzie's terror of heights.

McKenzie nodded at her friends, trying not to shake the bridge too much. Just hold on, put one foot in front of the other and everything will be fine. She took another step, then another.

By the time she was out in the middle, the bridge had dipped so much that she'd have to crawl her way uphill. She dropped to her knees and held onto the bridge for dear life. She shut her eyes and thought of Aidan and Lilicat just a few feet above her. She had to go forward. She couldn't go back.

'You can do it, Mack!' Aidan called.

That gave her courage and she pulled herself along a little farther. The farther she went, the easier it became. Soon she could open her eyes, and then finally she was dragging herself along the last few inches.

As she touched solid ground, Lilicat broke into a cheer.

'I knew you could do it,' Aidan said, pulling her into his arms.

'Never again.' Mack's mouth was so dry that her voice came out in a croak.

'I think the exit is up that way,' Lilicat said, her voice echoing off the walls of the huge room. She pointed to a gleam of light at the end of a passageway, and they hurried toward it.

McKenzie's legs felt rubbery, but she kept up with Lilicat and Aidan and nearly fainted with relief as they emerged into the cheerful chaos of the midway.

'I've never been so glad to see sunshine in my life.' Aidan ruffled McKenzie's hair and laughed. 'You neither, I bet.'

Lilicat started to giggle. 'Oh, Mack, did you see the look on Aidan's face when he went down that chute? It was priceless!'

McKenzie didn't answer. She still felt flushed and a little dizzy. The Catacombs hadn't been fun for her at all.

Tony walked up, shading his eyes from the late afternoon sun. 'Was it that bad?' He watched, dismayed, as Lilicat wiped tears from her eyes.

'It was great,' Lilicat said. 'You have a very warped mind!'

Tony gave a theatrical bow. 'I'll take that as a compliment.'

'It's definitely the coolest ride I've ever been on,' Aidan said. 'That chute was the best. I'm going to have to come back and do it all again.'

McKenzie decided that Aidan had lost his mind.

'I liked the costumes on those actors who played the Lizard Men,' Lilicat went on enthusiastically. 'How do they make their tongues move like that?'

'They weren't costumes and they weren't actors,' Tony explained. 'They were holograms – that was one of my ideas.'

'Holograms?' said McKenzie, feeling a rush of relief. 'You mean, all those creatures in there – '

'That's right,' said Tony. 'Holograms.'

'How do they work?' Lilicat asked.

Tony grinned and put an arm around her. 'Can't tell. Trade secret.'

'Oh,' McKenzie said, suddenly understanding. 'So that explains the chapel I wound up in – there was a hologram in there too?'

'Chapel?' said Tony. 'What chapel?'

'The one with the torches and the altar.'

'Altar?' Tony looked bewildered. 'Are you sure that's what you saw?'

'Don't tease her, Tony,' said Lilicat.

'There were two big rocks, standing upright, and a third, flat across the top. And there was a hologram in there of a girl who looked like me, and – '

'And?'

'And she was being strangled,' McKenzie said, her voice breaking as the memory of the vision returned.

'There's no hologram like that down there.'

'But I saw it,' McKenzie said. 'And there was

this man who was following me – and he knew my name! How did you do that?'

'I don't know what you're talking about.'

'Come on, Tony, admit it was a hologram,' said Aidan. 'You don't have to put up a front with us.'

'I'm not putting up a front. I'm serious.'

'Sure, sure,' said Lilicat.

McKenzie's face fell. Much as she didn't want to, she believed Tony. 'You're telling the truth, aren't you.' It was a statement, not a question.

Tony shoved his hands into his pockets and looked down for a moment. 'I don't know what else to say,' he said quietly. 'I didn't design a hologram like that. I did the Lizard Men, and there's a giant spider down one of the other tunnels and a dancing skeleton in another. Plus I've set up a few mirrors that create weird reflections, but I swear I've never put in anything like what you're describing.'

Now Lilicat grew serious. 'You really aren't joking,' she said.

'The holograms aren't set up to follow people around,' said Tony. 'Lilicat, Aidan – were you guys followed by anyone?'

Lilicat and Aidan glanced at each other and

shook their heads. McKenzie shut her eyes as a jolt of nausea returned.

"Scuze us a minute,' Aidan said, gently steering Mack away from the others. 'Mack,' he said, 'you're the only one who saw the chapel room and had someone following you. Now maybe Tony really does have some sort of trick up his sleeve that he won't talk about. But could it have been one of your – you know – one of your visions down there?'

'I don't know.' McKenzie shook her head in confusion. Was the image of herself being strangled created by her special powers? What about the man who knew her name? Could he be the same man who'd gone after Andrea Smith? Or was he some kind of phantom, a warning of things to come?

'Are you going to be all right?' Aidan asked.

She nodded and walked back over to Lilicat and Tony. 'Sorry,' she said, 'I guess I have a very active imagination.'

Lilicat shot her a look, and McKenzie knew she didn't buy the excuse.

'Why don't we take a walk and try to calm down after all that excitement?' Aidan suggested.

'Good idea,' Lilicat said. She turned to Tony. 'Are you still going to eat with us?'

He took her hand. 'I sure am. We've got the best food you ever tasted here – well, the best amusement park food, anyway.'

The last thing McKenzie wanted just then was food, but she didn't say anything.

The foursome walked up the midway, trying to decide on which junk food would make the best dinner.

'I think I'll just have cotton candy,' Lilicat said, 'in three colors.'

Tony rolled his eyes. 'The fried chicken grabstand is pretty good.'

'All I know is, whatever I choose won't have a single tomato in it,' Lilicat said.

'How are your jobs at the Total Tomato working out?' Aidan asked rather loudly.

'Fine,' Lilicat snapped.

'Aidan,' McKenzie said warningly. She'd told him that the last thing in the world Lilicat wanted was for Tony to see her in her uniform.

Aidan shot Lilicat a wicked glance and said, 'Listen, Tony, if you can get off for dinner some night, maybe we could visit Lilicat and Mack at the restaurant. The food is supposed to be pretty decent and – '

'Let's do it,' Tony said. 'I get sick of hot dogs.'

Lilicat's face took on an expression of pure panic. 'Our work schedules are pretty erratic,' she said quickly. 'Maybe you'd better wait until I know I'm working an evening.'

Aidan opened his mouth again and McKenzie punched him in the ribs.

'That's funny.' Aidan gripped McKenzie's wrist so she couldn't punch him again. 'Mack told me you're on a steady evening schedule with Fridays and Saturdays off.'

Lilicat stopped dead. She looked as if she didn't know whom to kill first. McKenzie shrugged her shoulders apologetically.

'What's going on?' Tony asked.

'Nothing,' McKenzie, Lilicat, and Aidan all said together.

Tony raised a skeptical brow. 'In that case, I wouldn't miss the Total Tomato for anything.' He winked at Lilicat. 'I'll stop by some evening.'

'Thanks, Aidan,' Lilicat said.

'Any time,' he assured her.

They decided on corn dogs and sausage sandwiches for dinner. McKenzie just drank a soda, which made her feel a little better. She noticed that whenever Lilicat wasn't gazing adoringly at Tony, she was glaring daggers at Aidan. The matter seemed to resolve itself when, after they'd eaten, Lilicat beat Aidan at the ring toss.

She won three stuffed animals; he won a six-inch ruler.

'We've got to do something else,' Aidan muttered after Lilicat won for the third time. He nodded down the midway toward a long tent covered with posters advertising a Giant, a Snake Woman, and other attractions.

'Step right up,' the barker cried. 'Finest show of its type in the Northeast. Freaks from all over the world. The most amazing collection ever to be assembled under one roof. Feast your eyes!'

'You can't miss the freak show,' said Tony, pulling the others toward the tent. 'It's one of our specialities.'

'I've always wanted to see one of those shows,' Aidan said. 'Let's go in.'

McKenzie followed Tony, Lilicat, and Aidan into the dim tent. The place was laid out like a maze. Each freak stood or sat in his own canvas booth. Gold-lettered signs outside each booth proclaimed what awaited inside.

Stretchman, 'The World's Tallest Man,' was in the first booth, his head skimming the tent's canvas roof. He juggled three eggs as Tony and Lilicat walked by.

'Nice work, Stretch. I see you've been practicing,' Tony said.

'Day and night,' the giant joked. His smile vanished as he caught sight of McKenzie, and the eggs he'd been juggling fell to the sawdust-covered floor. He turned his long, gaunt body away from them, and after a moment McKenzie and Aidan walked on.

They watched a short, bald man swallow fire in the next booth. Aidan seemed riveted by the performance, but McKenzie's mind was working overtime and she barely paid attention to the Fire Eater.

What on earth was going on? Stretchman acted as if he was afraid to see her. Maybe she'd startled him and he was embarrassed about dropping the eggs? She wasn't sure. But now that scary sensation that something was watching her, waiting for her to fall into its trap, had come back. It was really beginning to bother her. Maybe she was just being paranoid, but it sure felt real. McKenzie turned around quickly, jostling Aidan. 'I'm going on to the next booth,' she said, not willing to admit that standing in one place was making her feel like a target.

'Okay,' Aidan said, still fascinated by the Fire Eater. 'I'll catch up in a minute.'

McKenzie turned the corner, and at first she thought the next booth was empty. As she got closer, she saw that someone was in the booth after all. McKenzie looked over the divider and saw Shorty glowering up at her, his hands stuck in his front pockets. Relief coursed through her. She could handle being watched by the dwarf. Shorty might be temperamental, but she didn't think he was sinister. 'Hi, Shorty. What's the problem?' she asked.

Shorty didn't answer.

'You've been spying on me. I could tell Tony,' she went on, hoping her bluff would work.

Shorty inched closer to the front of the booth. He motioned for McKenzie to lean down a little. 'Leave Tony out of it,' he whispered. 'If you know what's good for you, you'll leave the park now and never come back.'

'Why?' McKenzie asked. 'I haven't done anything.'

Shorty glanced around him, although he couldn't possibly see over the pen. He leaned close again. 'Skip the rest of the show.'

'Not until you tell me why.'

Shorty wouldn't answer. He moved back and stood still as a statue as Aidan walked up to McKenzie and peered into the booth.

Aidan got a very uncomfortable look on his

face as he stared down at the misshapen little man. He took McKenzie's arm. 'Let's go.'

'What's wrong?' McKenzie asked when they were well away from Shorty.

'I felt funny staring at him, like he was an animal or something.'

McKenzie knew how he felt. She wasn't crazy about the freak show for more than one reason. Even though the freaks were all being paid for what they did, there was something about the way they were on display that seemed cruel.

'It's different with a guy like the Fire Eater,' Aidan said, still troubled. 'He's showing a skill, something he chose. But that dwarf – he was just born that way.' Aidan went on to the next booth. ' "Elijah, the Tattooed Man," ' he read. ' "Over 1,000 hours of work have gone into his tattoos." '

'That's the guy we applied to for summer jobs,' McKenzie whispered.

Aidan gave a low whistle. 'Must have been one strange interview.'

Before them, Elijah turned slowly, arms held away from his body so they could examine his tattoos. As he turned to face them, he gave McKenzie an inscrutable look.

'What do you think?' Aidan kidded as soon

as they were out of earshot. 'Maybe I should get tattooed like that.'

'Definitely,' McKenzie said. 'You could start with a big red and gold heart across your chest that reads, "McKenzie Forever." Then one on your arm that says, "I Love Gold," and you could put a real cute little one on your – '

Aidan pulled her against him and tickled her. 'It's a deal,' he said, making her laugh helplessly, 'as long as you get one that reads, "Aidan Collins is the best ever!" '

McKenzie pulled free. 'You egomaniac,' she said, still giggling. 'My tattoo will read, "Aidan Collins is a lunatic" ' – she stood on her toes and brushed his cheek with a kiss – ' "but I love him anyway." '

The second to the last booth was enclosed in glass. A woman sat inside wearing a gold lamé bikini and a python around her neck. The python reared up when McKenzie and Aidan came to the glass. Watching them with angry eyes, it struck at the glass suddenly. And the woman stared at McKenzie as if she'd seen a ghost.

'Unreal,' Aidan said.

They moved on quickly. Tony and Lilicat were silhouetted in the light of the exit. They were holding hands, and Lilicat was laughing at something Tony had said. McKenzie felt an unusual twinge of envy. Lilicat looked so carefree. McKenzie, on the other hand, had been joking around with Aidan, trying to pretend that nothing was wrong, but her heart was pounding madly. She just knew that something terrible was about to happen.

The last booth was covered by a red velvet curtain. A neatly lettered sign read, 'Pull this cord to see Dinah, the fattest woman in the world.'

Now McKenzie's heart beat even faster. Something told her to run away from the freak show, to take Shorty's advice and leave the park as fast as she could. But at the same time she was rooted to the spot, unable to move. Before she could do anything, Aidan pulled the cord.

The curtain parted to reveal a fat lady who filled the small booth. She was dressed in pigtails and a pinafore, a grotesque parody of a little girl.

How awful, McKenzie thought as she was flooded by a sudden sense of recognition.

The fat woman leaned forward, her pudgy hands tightening on the arms of her chair, the fat on her upper arms bulging and rippling. Her massive upper body was covered by a pale pink pinafore, and her thighs strained at the seams of white lace leggings. Her fading red hair was pulled into two scrawny pigtails.

'I'm Dinah!' announced the huge woman, leering at McKenzie.

Suddenly it hit her. McKenzie could hear the voice in her mind as she stared at the woman. 'Someone's in the kitchen with Dinah . . .'

She gasped. Dinah was real!

The Fat Lady's eyes met McKenzie's. Above her shoulder two carved wooden faces screamed in horror at something only they could see. McKenzie studied the pigtails and little girl clothing in fascinated disbelief. No one could have looked less like a baby doll. Or have felt less like one. She's furious, McKenzie realized. I've never seen anyone so angry.

McKenzie shut her eyes, suddenly dizzy – then terrified as she realized that the dizziness had somehow come from Dinah. She forced her eyes open. The Fat Lady stared at her with something like hate. Hate and awareness. As if the woman knew some secret about McKenzie.

The realization struck McKenzie like a kick in the stomach. Dinah was psychic. And she knew how to use and control her ability.

McKenzie looked into Dinah's cruel eyes and thought, 'Why do you hate me?' It was one of the few times she'd ever tried to use her power to send a thought to someone.

The Fat Lady narrowed her eyes, and leaned forward as if she'd get out of the chair. Her thought came back with startling force, 'I'm going to destroy you, McKenzie Gold. You don't have a chance against me.'

CHAPTER 9

McKenzie reeled with the force of Dinah's hate. Only one thought struggled against the Fat Lady's power: I've got to get out of here – *now*.

Aidan put a hand on McKenzie's shoulder. 'I've seen enough.'

'Me, too,' McKenzie said, bolting out of the tent.

'Wait a minute,' Aidan said as they neared Tony and Lilicat. He took hold of her arm. 'Are you all right? You were acting a little spacey in there.' He stroked her hair. 'Are you still shaken up from crossing that bridge?'

'A little,' McKenzie answered. She wondered what Aidan would say if she told him a dwarf had threatened her and the Fat Lady was a psychic who hated her? At last she said, 'I have a feeling something's wrong here, and it's all tied up with that girl who almost drowned the other day. I know the police think it was an accident, but I don't.'

Aidan put his arm around her. 'You had a rough time in the Catacombs today. How about we get out of here? Didn't you want to see the new Julia Roberts movie? It's at the Quad.'

McKenzie hesitated. Something was still terribly wrong at Idlewood, and she was reluctant to let it drop, at least not until she found out more about Dinah. 'I've – ' she began.

'We've been waiting for you two forever,' Lilicat interrupted, taking both Aidan and McKenzie by the arm and tugging them away from the tent.

'What did you think of the sideshow?' Tony asked them. 'It's pretty wild, isn't it?'

'It's wild all right,' said Aidan, putting an arm around McKenzie's shoulder. 'And creepy. Those freaks weren't exactly what I'd call friendly.'

'The freaks are a strange group,' Tony said. 'Most of them have been outcasts all their lives. When I try to talk with them, it's like there's always a wall between us. I don't think they really trust anyone except each other.'

'The tall man seemed okay,' Lilicat said. 'He smiled at me when I went past.'

'Stretch is definitely the friendliest,' Tony agreed. 'He may look intimidating, but he's as gentle as they come.'

'Enough about the sideshow,' said Lilicat. 'I want to ride the Ferris wheel. Come on, McKenzie – you can't keep putting it off!'

McKenzie saw Aidan's eyes light up at the suggestion, then grow serious as he looked at her. 'You up for this?' he asked.

'Not really,' McKenzie replied. 'You go ahead. I'll just walk around a little.' Before he could ask any questions, she turned to Lilicat and said, 'I'm going to wimp out on the Ferris wheel, but I know Aidan's dying to go. Would it be okay if he rides with you?'

'As long as he promises to behave,' Lilicat teased.

Aidan held up his right hand in a pledge. 'You won't even know I'm there.'

'Let's meet in front of the food concessions in twenty minutes.'

They all agreed. McKenzie watched them go through the ticket taker's gate and settle into a cab on the Ferris wheel. She started down the midway, looking for a game that might distract her, but her mind kept drifting back to the freak show. She shivered. She didn't want to go back there, ever, and yet . . . something seemed to call her back. She found herself walking toward it and stopped. No, she thought, I don't want to go back there! But something was pulling her, and she couldn't get away from it.

She slipped into the tent and walked quickly through the narrow aisles, heading straight for the Fat Lady.

Dinah's curtain was closed. McKenzie took a deep breath and pulled hard.

The chair was empty.

Dinah must have gone out a back way, McKenzie realized. She ran out the exit and around to the back of the tent. The back flap was untied, but the Fat Lady was nowhere to be seen. She could have disappeared into any of the trailers that lay behind the freak show tent.

McKenzie felt a little funny about entering such a private area, but she couldn't turn back now. She walked between a pair of long, silver Airstream trailers. 'Shorty' was lettered on the door of one. The other had a mailbox with 'Doris Berman' on it, and a wrought-iron image of a gypsy leaning over a crystal ball. Madame Beaupree's real name was Doris Berman?

McKenzie suppressed a nervous giggle. The freaks were taking on a whole different aspect.

Darkness was falling, and an eerie quiet cloaked the miniature trailer park.

A door closed down the aisle to McKenzie's left. She walked toward the sound, cinders crunching beneath her feet. She stopped outside a trailer that looked no different from the others. There was no name on the mailbox, but McKenzie knew who lived there. The force of Dinah's power radiated from the trailer like waves of evil.

McKenzie knew she had to enter the trailer, in the same way she'd known she had to go into the Catacombs.

She walked up the metal steps, and took a deep breath. Then she lifted her hand to rap on the door.

'Come in, Miss Gold.' No one had actually spoken, but Dinah's voice sounded in McKenzie's mind with astonishing clarity. A warning ran through McKenzie like a jolt of electricity.

She opened the door. The trailer was dark, and yet McKenzie felt like an animal pinned by the headlights of an oncoming car. When her eyes adjusted she saw Dinah sitting on a bench at the far end of the room.

'Come in.'

McKenzie stepped into the narrow trailer and walked past a rumpled bed that looked too small to hold the Fat Lady. She stopped at the end of the bed, a few feet from Dinah. The air almost crackled with the power emanating from the huge woman. The scent of stale incense tickled McKenzie's throat.

'I've been waiting for you.' The Fat Lady's watchful, malevolent eyes were surrounded by puffy welts of flesh. 'What kept you so long?'

McKenzie stared at her, bewildered. Beneath an open robe, Dinah was still dressed like a baby doll, with the face of a woman in her fifties. How old *was* she, McKenzie wondered.

'Fifty-one, to be exact.' Bitterness roughened Dinah's voice. 'And this idiotic costume is what I'm required to wear as part of the show.'

McKenzie forced herself to stand straight and look Dinah in the eye. The tickle in her throat made her cough, then stammer slightly. 'How do you know my name?' she managed.

The woman looked McKenzie up and down, as if taking her measure. 'Curiosity killed the cat,' she said softly.

'Why are you always watching me?' McKenzie asked, ignoring the remark. 'What do you want?'

'Guess.'

I can't let her see I'm afraid, McKenzie thought. She stood a little straighter. 'All right,' she said, 'I know you've got special powers. And I know you're connected to the girl who almost drowned.'

Dinah smiled. 'What do you think happened to her?'

An image returned to McKenzie of a man whose rotting, blue-gray flesh peeled from his body, revealing bone; whose lipless mouth leered hideously; whose eye, ready to fall from its socket, stared at her hungrily.

'*He* was the one who caught hold of her in the Tunnel?' McKenzie asked, horrified.

'He *didn't* get her. That's the problem.'

'Who is he?'

Dinah shrugged. 'He doesn't have a name.'

'You work for him,' McKenzie said, suddenly as sure of it as she was of her own name.

'You're a busybody,' Dinah said flatly. 'And it's going to get you killed.'

'You're afraid of me,' McKenzie returned. She was bluffing, but the expression in the Fat Lady's eyes told her that she was also right. 'And,' McKenzie went on slowly, 'you're afraid of him.'

'Anyone with any sense is afraid of Him.'

'Who is he?' McKenzie repeated. 'You know I'll find out.'

'Will you?' Dinah asked, her voice silky and menacing.

Even though the image terrified her, McKenzie forced herself to call it up again. She forced herself to look at the rotting blue flesh, at the dangling eye. She forced herself to look straight at him to see what he really was. He had died long ago, that much was obvious, and yet something in him had never died. McKenzie's heart began to pound as she sensed the thing that kept him alive – an overwhelming hunger, a hunger that could only be satisfied by blood . . . .

The Fat Lady squirmed on her bench. 'Don't *do* that!' It was almost a scream. 'Do you want to bring Him here?'

CHAPTER 10

Seconds ticked by as Dinah and McKenzie stared at each other. McKenzie shuddered, feeling an unexpected link with Dinah, a link forged by something outside of themselves, something too awful to think about.

The vision of the man was gone, but the walls of the trailer seemed to press in on McKenzie. Every time she breathed, stale, sweet incense clogged her lungs. She had to get outside *now*.

McKenzie stepped backward as the Fat Lady heaved to her feet and grabbed for her. A second later McKenzie was out the door, down the concrete steps, and rushing down the cinder alley. She ran past Shorty's trailer, made a quick right, swerved around the rear corner of the freak show tent, and found herself back in the main area of the park.

A throng of people surrounded her. The park was definitely more crowded. She hoped her friends would be waiting for her.

Slowly, as she made her way toward the food concessions, McKenzie felt herself returning to reality. She couldn't have been in Dinah's trailer for more than a couple of minutes, but it felt like hours. She remembered the vision of the carousel. The ghoulish figure in that vision was the same one she'd just seen. Who was he and how was he connected to Dinah and the runaway girl? There were so many unanswered questions – but finding the answers was dangerous. The more she found out, the more frightened she became.

She spotted her friends at a picnic table near the corn dog stand. Aidan shifted his legs and pulled her down beside him. McKenzie felt a wave of relief go through her at his warm touch.

'Will you look at this?' Aidan said, gesturing to seven corn dog sticks and three greasy French fry containers piled in front of Lilicat. The areas in front of Tony and Aidan were scrupulously clean. 'Lilicat ate it all.'

'Where do you put it?' Tony asked, his brown eyes shining with laughter.

'Thank God you're back, Mack,' Lilicat said. 'These two have been driving me crazy.'

McKenzie laughed a little shakily. Her heart was just starting to slow down.

'So what did you do without us?' Tony asked.

'I went to see Madame Beaupree again,' McKenzie answered, unwilling to tell him what had happened.

'What did she predict this time?' Lilicat asked.

'Great good fortune.' McKenzie smiled. 'That I'd go to a movie with a tall, handsome blond this evening.' She hoped Aidan would take the hint; she wanted to get out of Idlewood as soon as possible.

'How about something to eat first?' Aidan asked.

She shook her head. 'I'm not hungry, thanks. And if we leave now, we can make the seven o'clock show.'

Tony couldn't leave the park, but he said he'd drive Lilicat home later if she wanted to stay, and she gladly agreed.

McKenzie felt better as soon as she got into Aidan's car and they left Idlewood. She didn't say much, though. Her mind was on Dinah.

Somehow she had to find out more about her. The Fat Lady was the key to whatever was going on at Idlewood Park.

Dinah made her way to Madame Beaupree's tent in the dark of night. For a huge woman, she could walk quietly. She kept to the shadows when she passed the night watchman's post, knowing he'd never hear her over the wind.

Dinah stopped outside Madame Beaupree's tent, sensing the tension of the others gathered inside. Let them wait. Let their fear build. It was the only way she could be sure they'd obey her. It was the only way she could be sure they'd stop McKenzie Gold.

And she had to stop McKenzie. What she'd seen in her trailer had scared her. She'd known from the start that making contact with Him was always risky. There was always the possibility that He'd be drawn out of the Catacombs. And today He almost had been. The girl's powers were strong enough to conjure Him and set Him loose. Only Dinah could make sure the girl was stopped before she put them all in danger.

The girl reminded Dinah of herself long ago. The woman ran her hand through her thinning red hair. It was dyed and coarse now, but it used to be thick and flowing, just like McKenzie's. She'd been beautiful, too, running wild in the West Virginia hills. A poor life, but she'd had her brothers and sisters, and she'd had her future husband all picked out.

And then came the day Pa had discovered something unusual about his eldest daughter. She had the Sight. And from that day on he said no one was good enough for his Dinah.

He kept her a virtual prisoner at home for three years, trying to get her to use the Sight for his own purposes. Dinah rebelled the only way she could, by eating and eating until she was so repellent even Pa couldn't stand to look at her.

Finally she packed her bags and joined a carnival that was passing through. There, her only known talent was being fat. She kept the Sight to herself.

It had been a long haul from that rinky-dink carnival to Idlewood. Over the years she'd learned to use the Sight and control it. Now it was the one thing that could save them all from destruction.

Dinah pushed open the tent flap and gazed at the gathering of freaks. The fear on their faces pleased her; she would use it for their own good and hers. Some of them, like Elijah, hid their emotions well. But his calm expression didn't fool her; she could sense his terror as easily as she could see his tattoos.

She let the fear build like a wave as she slowly made her way to the chair they reserved for her.

The Snake Woman ran a hand along the glistening scales of the python draped around her neck.

Madame Beaupree stood stock-still, as if paralyzed. Her fortune-teller's crystal ball sat covered on a table in the center of the tent, just as Dinah had instructed.

Dinah looked at Elijah and said, 'I thought you were going to scare off McKenzie Gold.'

'I had the Strong Man follow her through the Catacombs,' Elijah answered, his voice shaking. 'He called her name. He warned her. He led her . . .'

'Right to the altar,' Dinah thundered. 'She saw what lay in store for her. And even that didn't scare her off!'

Everyone in the room seemed to have stopped breathing.

'I don't think you understand what this means,' Dinah went on. 'Idlewood is our home – our whole lives. Am I wrong? Perhaps some of you would like to leave the sideshow and live on the outside.' She looked each of the freaks in the eye, one by one. In every face she saw terror.

'That's what I thought. You all need this place. If it went under, where would you go? To the streets? To an insane asylum?'

Madame Beaupree whimpered. Even the Strong Man shook nervously. Dinah was pleased with the effect she was having on them. She went on.

'If we don't keep Him happy, He will escape from the Catacombs and run rampant through the park. You will have nowhere to go – *if* you get out alive.'

She paused, then continued. 'Some of you haven't been here that long. You don't remember what it used to be like. When I first came to Idlewood, the park had a history – young girls who mysteriously vanished. But I alone could see Him.' She shuddered as she remembered that first vision of decaying flesh. 'I didn't know what He was. All I knew was that He lived in the Catacombs and He was hungry.' Her eyes flickered to Shorty. 'Why don't you tell them what happened next?'

Shorty stared at the ground and shook his head.

'Then I'll tell them,' Dinah said. 'Shorty's sister came to visit Idlewood. She was sixteen. I told her to stay away from the Catacombs, but she didn't listen, and He took her. They never found her body.'

Shorty groaned and bolted from the tent.

'I understood then,' Dinah went on, 'that I had to find a way to keep us safe from Him. I learned to summon Him, to hear His thoughts. I promised that we would feed Him, and He agreed to remain in the Catacombs, to leave us alone. So far it has been a good . . . arrangement. But now – the runaway's escaped and He's hungrier than ever.'

Dinah stopped speaking as a white-faced Shorty slipped back into the tent and sat on the ground.

Tonight she'd show them, once and for all, what would happen to anyone who crossed her. 'If we don't feed Him, He will come out and take one of us to satisfy His hunger,' she said. 'You all know this. And yet you fail to obey my commands. Remember, my friends, the norms are here only until midnight. And it's *after midnight* that He walks!'

Dinah waved her hand at the tent flap. The wind blew the flap inward, as if someone – or something – waited outside.

Stretchman and the Snake Woman jerked around to stare at the tent flap. Shorty jumped to his feet, as if ready to fight. Madame Beaupree gasped and clasped her hands to her chest. Elijah and the Strong Man stood tall, but Dinah noted the goose bumps on their arms.

'Uncover your crystal, fortune-teller,' she said.

Madame Beaupree slid the cloth from the crystal ball.

'Look into the crystal,' Dinah commanded. She opened her eyes, gazed into its depths, and concentrated, knowing their fear would draw Him. Though she thought she was in control, she still couldn't stop a prickle of her own fear. This was the first time she'd ever called Him forth out of the Catacombs. She knew how dangerous that was. But she had to show them why it was so important to get McKenzie Gold for Him. She had to remind them how hungry He was.

She pictured His rotting face. His eye, dripping pus. His grayish flesh and lipless mouth.

At first she had to force herself to remember the details of His appearance. Then, almost before she realized it, she was looking into His eyes with her mind. He was below, in the Catacombs.

'Come forth.' She spoke to Him aloud so the others could hear. 'Enter the crystal and reveal yourself.'

He didn't answer, and for a frantic moment she wondered if He wouldn't obey, if somehow she'd lost the power to command Him. Then something shimmered within the crystal. A grayish blue hand appeared. Disappeared. Appeared.

The rest of Him followed quickly. The stench of rotting meat filled the tent.

Madame Beaupree gasped and Elijah yanked a pistol from his pocket.

The creature turned to Dinah with a toothless grin and snickered. 'Which one?'

'Take your pick,' Dinah answered. The freaks were quaking. They'd never disagree with her again.

'No, Dinah!' begged Elijah. 'We tried to get the runaway. We tried to scare off that other girl. We've done everything you asked. Please don't punish us!'

'Hunger,' groaned the spirit.

Even the wind outside seemed to still in order to hear who would be chosen. He turned slowly. His putrid eye passing over each of the freaks. Tears of sheer fright rolled down Madame Beaupree's face. The Snake Woman shivered. Shorty and Stretch clutched each other, and Elijah and the Strong Man couldn't help but look away from the horrid monster. Dinah enjoyed this spectacle of fear. Then she felt His eyes on her.

'Feed me!' he rasped.

But Dinah wasn't about to provide Him with a meal now. She'd only intended to frighten the others into submission – and that, judging by the looks on their faces, she'd done. Dinah looked into the crystal again and willed the creature to return to the Catacombs. She pictured Him there among the rocks and twisting passageways.

'No!' he said. His image remained clear within the crystal.

Dinah began to panic. What happened next should not have happened.

The spirit reached out, and His arm passed through the surface of the crystal ball as if it were water. The blue-gray flesh reached toward the Snake Woman. She screamed and lunged sideways, but not quickly enough. His grotesque hand closed around the python. The snake disappeared along with His arm back into the crystal.

The Strong Man ran over to help the Snake Woman, who knelt on the floor sobbing.

'My baby, my baby,' she repeated over and over, rocking back and forth.

'He had to be fed,' Dinah said, trying to hide her own shock. He shouldn't have been able to reach outside the crystal, but He had. Nothing had prepared her for that. She glanced over the group, her own heart pounding. She had to keep control. 'You lost the runaway,' she told them sternly. 'And today you had your chance to scare McKenzie Gold. But you failed. I told you we had to get rid of her, and you didn't listen. Now you've seen what He can do. How much more proof do you need?'

'She's right,' Madame Beaupree said, her face a ghastly shade of white beneath her makeup. 'We can't let Him come back.'

Gradually, Dinah felt her pulse return to normal, but the fear hadn't left her. She had to get back to her trailer and think. She looked around the tent again. The others didn't know something had gone wrong, which was exactly as it should be.

She stood up and walked slowly to the open tent flap. 'No more questions,' she said. 'Kill McKenzie Gold.'

CHAPTER 11

All day Saturday, as McKenzie served Tomato Delights and stuffed tomatoes, she added up everything she knew about Idlewood Park: the drowning girl, the vision of herself being strangled in the Catacombs, Dinah's psychic powers. She glanced at the tomato-filled food blender. Not to mention her vision of the carousel and the awful thing that had offered her a ride. What did it all add up to?

Murder?

Lilicat slapped a towel down on the stainless steel counter. 'Okay, Mack. I've been dying of curiosity all day and I can't take it anymore. Spill it.'

McKenzie didn't know where to start.

'It's about Idlewood,' Lilicat prompted.

McKenzie nodded. 'There's something about Dinah . . .'

'Who?'

'The Fat Lady.' McKenzie told Lilicat about her encounter with Dinah in her trailer.

'Do you think she tried to drown that girl?'

'No. She wasn't anywhere near the Tunnel of Love.' McKenzie wiped up some spilled tomato juice. A new idea occurred to her. 'But one of the other freaks could have been.'

Lilicat nodded. 'Why?'

'That's the question I can't answer yet. I think I need to talk to Tony. Maybe he can help.'

Lilicat sighed dreamily. 'He's coming over tonight with a pizza. Mom's got a date and I bribed Gillian to stay in her room.'

'Would you mind—?' McKenzie didn't even need to finish her sentence.

'No problem. I can tell all of this is driving you crazy. Tony will be at my house around eight. Bring Aidan if you want.'

'I think he has to work late,' McKenzie said, 'but I'll ask him.'

The wind gusted as McKenzie ran up the walk to Lilicat's house. Darkness had just fallen, and raindrops the size of quarters splattered on the concrete. McKenzie let herself in as lightning streaked the sky.

'Come on in!' Lilicat called. She and Tony were in the living room, sprawled on the carpet, working on a large pizza. 'Grab a slice!' she said, over a roll of thunder.

McKenzie helped herself to a slice of pizza, glad to be inside the cozy house. The three of them ate for a while, talking easily about their jobs.

'At least you get to work in an amusement park,' Lilicat said to Tony. 'Idlewood's got to be more interesting than the Total Tomato.'

'I love the park,' Tony said. 'But it's got plenty of problems. There's an unwritten rule – at least one ride per day must break down. I seem to spend a lot of time fixing things or finding someone else to fix them – not exactly a thrill a minute.'

'But what about the people?' McKenzie asked. 'What's it like to work with the freaks?'

'It's funny,' Tony said. 'When I was a little kid I used to hang out in their trailers all the time – especially Stretch's. They made me their unofficial mascot. We even used to put on shows together. Shorty and I would play Siamese twins.'

Lilicat laughed. 'I guess you were just his size back then.'

Tony smiled and nodded, but his face was a little sad. 'They were great childhood play-mates. But when I got older they began to shut me out – and now they pretty much keep to themselves.' He stretched out on the floor, lean-ing on one arm. 'I guess I shouldn't be surprised by it. In some ways their world is the opposite of ours.'

'What do you mean?' Lilicat asked.

'In our world a dwarf or a grotesquely fat person is sneered at or pitied. But in the freaks' world, those types rule. They have more status than, say, a performer like Madame Beaupree.'

Thunder burst, sounding as if it were directly over the house. The electric candles in the chandelier flickered, and the lamp swung from side to side, throwing long shadows against the wall.

'They've always fascinated me,' Tony con-tinued. 'When I was a kid I used to tell my father I wanted to be a freak. Now I hate to use that word, even though they insist on it.'

'You work with them every day,' said McKenzie. 'Aren't you close to any of them anymore?'

'With the freaks, you never get too close

unless you're one of them,' Tony answered. 'When I grew up, I became the enemy. I'm the owner's son, and they resent Idlewood and my dad because they're so dependent on it. There are so few parks with real sideshows anymore. Those guys have a terrible time in the outside world. Idlewood is their whole life.'

Lightning flashed and the lights flickered again.

'What about Dinah?' Lilicat asked. 'Do you know much about her?'

Tony shrugged. 'She's quiet about her past. Most freaks are. I think she's from West Virginia. She's been at Idlewood about ten years.'

'Is she their queen bee?' asked McKenzie.

'I guess so. She's got the strongest personality. She and I have never really gotten along,' Tony admitted. 'She always seems to have a chip on her shoulder.'

To say the least, McKenzie thought. Tony didn't seem to know anything about Dinah's psychic abilities.

Lilicat set her plate aside, and moved closer to Tony. 'When that girl almost drowned last week, I heard people talking about other accidents at the park.'

'There are always accidents at amusement parks,' said Tony. 'I mean, last summer we had a ten-year-old boy who decided to body surf down the log flume, and another kid who wound up dangling off one of the seats on the Ferris wheel. This stuff happens all the time.' He reached up to rub Lilicat's shoulders gently. 'There's even a legend about the old Catacombs that sort of explains some of the accidents.'

Thunder crashed. Lilicat waited until it died away before asking, 'Well?'

'I guess it's the perfect night for a ghost story.' Tony leaned back against the couch. 'About a hundred years ago there was a mine where Idlewood is now. The mine ran about a half mile down under the hills at the back of the park.'

'The Catacombs,' Lilicat whispered.

Tony nodded. 'Most of those tunnels were ready-made for us by the miners. Around the turn of the century one of the tunnels collapsed. Twelve men were trapped beneath the rubble. Eleven were rescued. Only the foreman of the crew didn't make it.'

'That's terrible,' McKenzie said. 'Why couldn't they get him out?'

'By some accounts they just couldn't reach him. By others, they didn't want to.'

A bolt of lightning lit the skies, and the filaments on the chandelier's electric candles glowed orange for a few seconds, then faded away to black. The room plunged into darkness.

Lilicat pulled a curtain aside and looked out. Rain streamed down the windows. 'The lights are out all up and down the street,' she reported. 'I'll get a candle.'

Tony and McKenzie sat listening to the noise of the storm outside.

Footsteps sounded on the hall stairs and a dark shape darted into the room. 'Where is everybody?'

McKenzie recognized Lilicat's twelve-year-old sister, Gillian. Gillian was usually very self-assured, but tonight she sounded young and a little frightened.

'We're over here,' Tony called. 'Don't step on the pizza.'

The dark shape stepped closer. McKenzie's eyes were starting to adjust to the darkness. 'Hi, Gillian.'

'Hey, Mack. So where's the dwarf?'

McKenzie was startled until she realized the girl had found another nickname for Lilicat, whom she topped by several inches. 'Getting a candle. Spooky, huh?'

'Yeah. Could you pass me a plate? I might as well have some pizza.'

Lilicat walked back into the room, shielding a candle with one hand. She set the candle on the coffee table. It lit their faces as if they were gathered around a campfire. 'We're set,' she said. 'Let's get back to the story.'

'Why wouldn't they rescue the foreman?' McKenzie asked.

'They say he fired one of his men for skipping work on the day his wife was giving birth,' Tony continued. 'And the man was so poor he couldn't afford a doctor or midwife. It turned out that his wife had a bad delivery, and if he hadn't been there, she would have died. He was a really tough boss.

'Anyway, a few minutes after all the men were out of the tunnel that had collapsed, the main shaft caved in. The miners considered themselves lucky – only one fatality among a hundred and fifty men. Then the screams started. The foreman wasn't dead. He was just badly injured. And now he was trapped beneath the rubble.'

Buried alive, McKenzie thought.

'He screamed for two days,' said Tony. 'He pleaded for help, but no one would risk his own life to rescue the guy. He kept yelling, begging for help, telling them that he was hungry, that he was starving to death. Then the screams stopped and they could hear him moaning. It went on that way for nearly a week. Eventually the moans stopped.'

'I'm not so sure I'll visit the Catacombs again,' Lilicat said with a shudder.

McKenzie didn't say anything. Tony's words, '. . . *he was hungry . . . he was starving to death,*' rang in her head like alarm bells.

'The tunnels are safe now,' Tony said, pulling Lilicat close to him. 'All rebuilt and reinforced. Anyway, the story is that the miner's out for revenge. They say his spirit still haunts the park, taking human sacrifices every so often to slake his thirst for vengeance.'

Lilicat's mouth hung open, and McKenzie had a feeling she looked just as frightened.

'Do you hear something?' Gillian whispered.

'Speak up,' Lilicat said. 'The thunder's so loud we can hardly hear you.'

'I said, do you hear something?' Gillian's words came out unnaturally loud in the silence between crashes of thunder.

Everyone stopped talking and listened. All they heard was the hiss of rain and the roar of thunder.

'You guys don't believe in ghosts, do you?' Tony asked. He laughed. 'That's just an old story. Sometimes I think my father made it up to give the park a spooky atmosphere.'

McKenzie was silent, remembering her vision in Dinah's trailer of the rotting creature and the overwhelming hunger she'd felt coming from it. That grotesque thing had to be the spirit of the foreman.

CHAPTER 12

'**Hey, Gillian's right,**' said Lilicat, her eyes wide. 'I hear it, too. Someone's knocking on the door.'

'I'll go with you,' Tony said. He and Lilicat walked out into the hallway. McKenzie didn't hear the front door open. They were probably just looking through the peephole. A few seconds later Tony and Lilicat were back.

'No one there,' Lilicat said. 'I think that story has me spooked.' She and Tony sat down again.

Gillian still looked a little doubtful, but she said, 'Hey, I know a good one about – '

Tap, tap, tap.

There was no doubt about it this time. Someone was knocking, but not on the door. The noise came from the window at Tony's back.

Tap, tap, tap.

Tony drew the curtain aside.

A flash of lightning illuminated a pale face pressed against the window, water running from its long hair into its eyes and down its cheeks.

Gillian shrieked.

Tony ran to the window and yanked it open.

'Close that thing!' Lilicat yelled.

McKenzie's heart gave one big thud and began to beat normally again. She'd have recognized that slightly crooked nose anywhere. 'Aidan!'

Lilicat, Tony, and Gillian all breathed sighs of relief as McKenzie ran to open the front door.

A dripping Aidan stood on the Caines' welcome mat. 'Boo!' He stepped inside, grinning. 'I got off early.'

'You almost scared us to death,' McKenzie said. She tried to look mean, but couldn't help smiling. 'You'll get no mercy from me, Collins.'

'Show me none.' He leaned down and gave her a long kiss. A trickle of water fell from his hair onto her face.

Lilicat brought him a towel to dry off with. 'Sorry, I can't offer you dry clothes,' she said. 'We don't have anything that would fit you. Guess you'll just have to sit there in your wet stuff.' She flashed him a wicked grin. 'And it serves you right.'

'It's a good thing none of us had a gun,' Tony said. 'You'd be history.' He clapped Aidan on the back, then drew his hand away, soaking wet. He grimaced. 'How long were you out there, anyway?'

'Too long. I kept knocking but no one answered. So I came around to the window and peeked in. There you all were, snug and dry.' Aidan pushed some hair from his forehead. 'I couldn't resist.'

'Try, next time,' McKenzie said.

'I'd better not stay. I'd probably catch pneumonia and not one of you would come to my funeral.'

'Can you blame us?' Lilicat asked. 'Tony was just telling us about the ghost that haunts Idlewood Park.'

Aidan glanced at McKenzie, understanding now why he'd scared them so badly. He sounded sincere as he said, 'I really am sorry if I scared you guys.'

McKenzie was ready to go home. Tony's story had given her a lot of the information she needed. Besides, she figured Lilicat and Tony might want to be alone. 'I'm on my way, too.'

They said good night and hurried to their cars through the rain.

'I have to work most of the day, so I'll call you tomorrow night, Mack,' Aidan said, kissing her lightly.

'I want a totally nonscary date with you,' McKenzie said, kissing him back.

'No problem,' Aidan murmured. 'We can do something exciting, like bake cookies.'

McKenzie pushed him away. 'You mean *I* can bake cookies. Last time *we* baked cookies, you played Nintendo with Jimmy.'

'I know,' Aidan said ruffling her hair. 'And remember how well they turned out? Me playing Nintendo is definitely the way to bake *great* cookies.'

McKenzie tossed in bed, unable to get Tony's story out of her head. The Catacombs were entangled with the old mine. Was it really the dead miner she'd seen in the carousel vision and in Dinah's trailer? She turned over restlessly for the fortieth time. Was he after her?

Cre-eeeeak.

McKenzie's door opened.

Blue, her black cat, ambled in. He jumped up on the bed and poked his nose at her cheek.

She rubbed his head as he lay down beside her. 'Time for bed, Blue?'

He purred.

McKenzie had an idea how she might find out if the miner legend was real. She switched on her lamp, then hopped out of bed and found the jeans she'd been wearing Friday.

She searched the right pocket. Yes, there it was. She pulled out the orange ticket stub she'd used to get into the Catacombs that day. The ticket was folded in half because it was bigger than the average ticket. The front showed a picture of the entrance to the Catacombs.

McKenzie got back into bed and lay down. She held the ticket stub in both hands and fixed her eyes on it, as if she were meditating. Nothing happened at first. She felt herself go deeper, concentrate harder.

The ticket stub warmed in her hands. As she stared at it, the entrance to the Catacombs seemed to become three-dimensional.

McKenzie felt herself standing in front of that entrance. And fear hit her like a tidal wave.

She forced herself to take the two steps that carried her into the tunnel. The cool air brushing by her face smelled like wet sand and rocks. McKenzie was engulfed by darkness, but somehow she could still see, as if the walls of the tunnel gave off a supernatural light.

Her feet didn't seem to touch the ground as she made her way down into the heart of the Catacombs.

She returned to the alcove where she'd seen an image of herself being strangled. And she found what she was looking for.

The thing from the carousel emerged from the alcove, stretching out a hand covered with emaciated gray flesh. One of his toes, eaten away almost to the bone, poked from the rotting leather of one of his boots. It was the miner, she was sure of it.

For a minute he seemed unaware of McKenzie. She followed his lurching steps with her own silent ones, curious and yet afraid to get too close.

Without warning the miner turned and stared right at her, one eyeball hanging partway from its socket. His chest seemed to rise and fall beneath the torn yellow overalls. How could someone – something – that had been dead so long breathe?

Most of his lips were eaten away, but he grinned as he stepped towards her.

McKenzie couldn't move.

There was something around his neck – a

partially-eaten python, whose bloody stump hung halfway down the miner's body.

Now the miner reached out to her. McKenzie tried to back away, but her legs were frozen.

The python reared up at McKenzie and opened its mouth, hissing.

CHAPTER 13

The snake's hissing jarred McKenzie back to reality. She swung her hand out in self-defense and just missed hitting Blue. The cat was arching his back and hissing at the center of the room. Nothing was there.

Had something been there? McKenzie wondered. Her heart hammered away in her chest. Was it the spirit from the mine? She dropped the Catacombs ticket, damp with sweat, on her bedside table.

A minute later Blue had calmed down a little. McKenzie stroked him until his tail stopped twitching and he closed his eyes. 'Good night, attack cat,' she murmured. But long after Blue fell asleep, she lay staring at the ceiling.

The next morning she woke to the smell of bacon frying. She dressed quickly in jeans and a T-shirt and ran a comb through her hair. If she wanted any of that bacon, she'd probably have to fight Jimmy for it.

'Good morning, everyone,' McKenzie said as she stepped into the sunny kitchen. Her family was gathered around the table, helping themselves to generous portions of eggs, bacon, and toast.

Cholesterol City, McKenzie thought. Mr. Berrian would be horrified.

'Good morning, McKenzie,' her father said. 'Some storm last night. Did the power go out at Lilicat's?'

'Yup. And Aidan scared us to death by peering in the window like a psycho.' McKenzie put a slice of toast down and then poured herself a cup of coffee from the drip-machine beneath the window. The sky today was clear and blue, washed clean by the storm. She wished she felt half as cheerful as the sky looked.

'Anyone else for coffee?' McKenzie asked. Her father nodded and she poured him another cup.

'No thanks, dear,' her mother said. She looked up from the newspaper she'd been glancing through. 'Are you coming down with something?' Mrs. Gold asked, frowning. 'You don't look well today.'

'I'm fine,' McKenzie said, sitting down at the table across from her father.

'At least you don't have to work today, Lazybones,' he said, smiling. He passed the bacon her way, and Jimmy grabbed a piece from the plate as it passed him.

McKenzie grinned at her father and began to feel better. It was Sunday and she had absolutely no plans. She could sit outside and read, maybe. Catch up on her diary entries.

As she thought about all the ways she could spend her day, she became aware of everyone's eyes on her. Including Jimmy's.

'McKenzie,' her mother said, 'I'd like you to watch Jimmy today. Your father and I are going to the store to finish the inventory.'

'Sure, I'll watch him,' McKenzie said. 'The inventory's not done yet?' She'd thought her father would have finished it yesterday, even though his assistant, Mabel, was still sick.

'We ought to be able to finish up today.' Shelby Gold smiled at his daughter. 'Meanwhile, we thought you might take Jimmy to the amusement park.'

Jimmy's eyes were fixed on McKenzie's expectantly.

Idlewood was the last place in the world she wanted to go. Just the thought of the place made her head ache. 'Let's do something else,' she said to her brother. 'I've already been to Idlewood twice in the last two weeks.'

'But I haven't been there at all this summer,' Jimmy protested. 'And I heard that new Catacombs ride is totally cool.'

'Honestly, Jimmy, it's not that great. It's not even a ride. You have to climb around in the dark,' McKenzie explained. 'Tell you what, it's so hot out, why don't we go to the lake today and we'll do Idlewood some other time?'

'Mack,' her mother said, 'would it be so terrible to go back to Idlewood just one more time?'

Yes it would! McKenzie wanted to scream, the vision of the miner clear in her mind.

'Please, Mack?' Jimmy's brown eyes were pleading.

McKenzie looked at her father. She had a feeling she wasn't going to be able to get out of this. But she had to take a stab at it.

Jimmy turned to Mrs. Gold. 'I said "please" and she still won't do it,' he said sorrowfully.

'We promised a week ago to take him, McKenzie,' her mother said. 'I shouldn't have promised him, but I didn't realize Mabel would be out all week.'

'I was just there yesterday,' McKenzie said.

She knew she was going to have to do better than that for an excuse. 'Look,' she said, 'a girl almost drowned in the Tunnel of Love last week. I don't think Idlewood is a safe place for anyone right now.' They were all looking at her blankly. She searched her brain desperately for the right words. 'What I'm trying to say is, there's something really dangerous going on there. I don't know what it is. If I did, I'd tell you. I'd call Officer Rizzuto. But I haven't figured it out and I just can't go back – and I can't be responsible for taking my little brother into that . . . that . . .'

'I'm not little!' Jimmy burst out, rolling his eyes. 'I'm eight!'

McKenzie held back a yelp of frustration.

'Okay, Mack, calm down,' her father soothed her. 'I'm not quite sure what's bothering you, but if you feel that strongly about it, then you can take Jimmy to the lake for the day instead.'

'Just as long as you remember to drop him off at Brian's by four o'clock,' Mrs. Gold added. 'He's sleeping over there. We won't be back till late, so leave us a note if you plan to go out.'

With a sigh of relief, McKenzie ran upstairs to change into her bathing suit. When she came back down, she heard her mother saying to Jimmy, 'I may have to time to take you myself tomorrow, if you help me out with the shopping in the morning.'

On the way to the lake, Jimmy didn't say much. But as soon as he saw some other boys riding the tire swing out over the lake and crashing into the water, his mood improved. And he was all too willing to talk when it was time for lunch.

'You should have brought Ring Dings, not peaches!' he exclaimed, totally exasperated.

'Just eat your baloney sandwich and cut the baloney!' McKenzie shot back, grinning at him as he gulped down his sandwich and half of hers.

'Hey, no swimming right after eating!' she called out as he dove into the water. Then she gave up and stretched out on her towel. If Jimmy wanted to get a stomach ache and ruin his own good time, that was just fine with her.

She'd try to salvage a tan out of this babysitting fiasco. At least I'm not at Idlewood, she thought. Anything's better than that.

But after a while she began to feel as if she was baking in an oven. She got up and wandered down to the lake to get her feet wet. Crouching down by the water's edge, she shielded her eyes with her hand and looked out over the sparkling silver surface. 'Jimmy!' she called out. 'Where are you?'

There was no answer. And then she saw him.

Beneath the water's surface.

His face loomed before her, excited, happy, smiling. And then it became twisted and contorted with terror. He was screaming silently, his open mouth a ghastly black hole, and there was nothing at all she could do . . . .

'No!' she screamed as a cold wave hit her back.

She swung around and stared at her laughing brother, who stood there clutching a child's green plastic pail, watching her shudder as rivulets of lake water coursed down her back.

'I'm going to get you for this!' she shouted. 'Get in the car right now!'

When they pulled up in front of Brian's house, she'd pretty much forgiven him. But a strange feeling nagged at her. Something was wrong, but she wasn't sure what it was. 'Don't make any trouble for Brian's mother,' she told him, pulling his Mets cap down over his eyes. 'You're *her* responsibility until tomorrow, God help her.'

Jimmy grinned and jumped out of the car. 'Bye!'

Dinah sat down heavily, facing the Seeing mirror. The freaks had their uses, but obviously it was up to her to find a way to eliminate McKenzie Gold. She gazed into the mirror, watching its clear reflection waver and then cloud over.

She focused on McKenzie Gold, chanting the girl's name over and over in a low monotone. She pictured the girl's intelligent gray-green eyes, her straight auburn hair, and the dusting of freckles across her nose.

She saw McKenzie and a small, curly-haired boy who looked to be about eight sitting in a car in front of a suburban house. The boy wore a Mets cap. McKenzie said something and yanked the brim of his cap down over his eyes, grinning. The boy turned the cap so it was backward, got out of the car, and ran toward the house.

How touching, Dinah thought. McKenzie and her little brother, perhaps? Both of them seemed to have wet hair.

McKenzie drove away, and though she concentrated on following her, Dinah found herself following the boy to the front porch of the house. Another little boy answered the door.

She began to hear voices, and she stopped

murmuring McKenzie's name so that she could hear.

'I ended up going to the lake today,' said the first boy. 'It was fun, but I really wanted to go to Idlewood.'

The boys went out into the backyard and climbed up into a tree house.

'I thought your sister was gonna take you,' the other boy said.

'She just won't do it,' the first little boy said gloomily. 'She says it's because she's been there twice already this summer, but I think it's because she's scared of the rides.'

'You got a weird sister, Jimmy.' The second boy picked up a rock and tossed it at a street sign. 'I've gone three times this week, but I'd definitely go again. The Catacombs is bad!'

'Hey, Brian, I've got an idea! Maybe your brother Richard would take us!' Jimmy said, straddling a sturdy branch.

Suddenly Brian looked excited, too. 'Yeah! Richard will take us!'

'I'll call my parents at the store and tell them,' said Jimmy. 'My mom will be psyched to get out of taking me tomorrow.'

Dinah chuckled to herself as she watched the boys scramble down from the tree house. Soon she was laughing so hard that the sound filled her small trailer. She had what she needed to get that meddlesome girl. It would be easy to lure McKenzie Gold back into Idlewood. She would lay a trap for her, with irresistible bait. McKenzie's dear little brother.

CHAPTER 14

McKenzie stood in front of her bedroom mirror, brushing out her long auburn hair. Blue hopped up on the dresser in front of her and butted his head against her chest.

McKenzie studied her reflection. 'Why am I bothering with my hair?' she asked the cat. 'Aidan is working again. Mom and Dad are still at the store, and even Jimmy is out. He'd better be behaving himself at Brian's.'

Blue put out a paw and batted at one of her perfume bottles.

McKenzie lifted her perfume out of the way and smiled down at the cat. 'At least *you're* not bored.'

Much to her surprise, she found herself wishing Jimmy was there to keep her company. Then again, maybe she ought to be grateful for having an evening to herself. She didn't get one that often. Maybe it was the Idlewood situation that was bothering her. She wasn't going to figure out what was wrong by avoiding the place. But the thought of going back was horrible. She'd only go if Lilicat dragged her there, which was bound to be soon, based on the way things seemed to be going between her and Tony.

She lifted her hair off her neck and held it up in a twist, wondering if it made her look devastatingly sophisticated. She turned her head, peered out the corner of her eye, and saw her brother gazing back at her.

'Jimmy?' McKenzie stared at his smiling reflection in the mirror, then turned around. Jimmy wasn't in the room behind her. But somehow he was in the mirror, his reflection as clear as her own.

Just as she'd seen him in the lake.

A shiver went through McKenzie. She leaned toward the mirror, and suddenly there wasn't just one Jimmy, there were dozens, each one looking tiny and far away. It was as if someone had cloned him again and again and again. The images kept multiplying until McKenzie was almost dizzy.

She shook her head, as if that would break

the vision. But her brother was still there, stretching out his hand to her. And there were still too many of his reflections.

Something was changing. Jimmy looked frightened. As if from miles away, she heard him scream in terror.

Dozens and dozens of Jimmies began to cry, tears running down their cheeks. And they all began to back away from something unseen.

McKenzie felt herself go hot then cold, as if she were feverish. She was certain this vision meant to tell her that Jimmy was in trouble somewhere.

She heard a sound over his crying, the sound of glass breaking. The pictures of Jimmy fragmented and dissolved like ice turning to water.

Now there was only her own reflection and the cat's in the mirror. Blue touched his nose to its silvery surface, leaving a small, damp smudge. Mirrors, McKenzie thought. Why did I see Jimmy in my mirror? Why so many reflections? And why was he so scared?

And then she understood. What she'd seen was her brother trapped in mirrors – the kind you'd find in a fun house hall of mirrors. Jimmy was trapped at Idlewood.

McKenzie grabbed the keys to her mother's

new Volvo, clattered down the front steps, and headed for Idlewood, pushing the speed limit as far as she dared. For once she was actually relieved when the roller coaster came into view.

Please be all right, Jimmy, she prayed as she got out of the car and began to race across the parking lot toward the gate.

By the time she reached the Fun House she was out of breath, but she couldn't stop. She ran past the ticket taker. 'Hey, we're closing!' he shouted.

McKenzie ignored him and ducked through the huge, grinning clown's mouth that was the door to the Fun House. She ran through the first two rooms, now darkened, past displays and figures that were shut down for the night.

She stopped in the third room and listened. A witch's eye gleamed at her evilly, lit by a stray moonbeam that had found its way through a chink in the walls.

Everything was quiet ahead. Of course, McKenzie thought, the way I ran into this place, I've probably alerted whoever was in here.

She walked quietly toward the entrance of the fourth room. Nothing moved in the darkness. McKenzie stepped through the doorway.

A floorboard creaked beneath her tennis shoes.

She stopped. The Hall of Mirrors was next. The place would be like a maze. She'd be lucky to find her way through it in the dark, let alone find Jimmy.

The room was lighter than she'd thought it would be. It glowed eerily.

The minute she stepped into the room, all she could see was her own reflection. A thousand McKenzies surrounded her, all white-faced.

She'd once read that, in a maze, it was best to choose one direction and just keep going that way. Right, she told herself, I'll just keep going to the right.

Someone sniffled and began to cry softly, and McKenzie forgot all about directions.

Jimmy. Like the images she'd seen of him earlier, the sound was fragmented and seemed to come from everywhere at once. Was her brother really here? She couldn't tell what she was seeing. Maybe a vision. Maybe a hologram. She didn't dare risk calling out.

She stopped when the sobbing got louder. Putting her hand on a glassy surface, she felt the mirror shake gently. Could Jimmy be on the other side, crying?

She pushed on the mirror, but it wouldn't give.

McKenzie couldn't rely on her eyes in the Hall of Mirrors because everywhere she saw her own frightened reflection running at her. She held her arms out to her sides, and when she felt a break in the line of mirrors she turned down the narrow corridor.

And then she saw him. Jimmy was somewhere ahead of her. There were dozens of reflections. He was wearing his Mets cap turned backward on his head.

'Jimmy!' she called, relief surging through her. She wasn't too late.

Her brother turned a tear-streaked face to her. 'Mack?'

A blue-green arm reached out from some hidden place and clamped itself tightly around the boy's neck. Then McKenzie watched in horror as all the images of Jimmy's terrified face disappeared.

CHAPTER 15

'Jimmy!' **McKenzie screamed**. 'Where are you?'

'Mack!'

She followed the sound of his voice, down a narrow passageway between the mirrors. Seconds later she walked smack into her own reflection. She rubbed her forehead, trying to hold back tears of panic. Jimmy was somewhere in here. If she could just stay calm, she'd find him.

She called his name again, and again he called back. This time his voice seemed to come from behind her. She turned, felt her way around a corner, and through another corridor. Was she going back the way she'd come? She couldn't even tell.

She blinked as she saw her own reflections

widen, each one squat, each one even fatter than Dinah. 'Jimmy!'

He called again, this time from the left.

Walking with her hands held out in front of her, she found a corridor to the left. McKenzie felt her heartbeat slow as she saw Jimmy's reflection at the end of the corridor.

She seemed to be near the end of the Hall of Mirrors. Before her was only one long aisle with mirrors on both sides and her brother's reflection at the very end.

McKenzie ran toward him, then stopped horrified as another reflection appeared in the mirror. It was a long, muscular, tatooed blue-green arm, holding an enormous club.

'No!' McKenzie raced up the aisle.

The club came crashing down. Mirrors shattered everywhere.

McKenzie stood amid the splinters of glass, sobbing. Jimmy was gone. There was no sign of him. Just an endless sea of mirrors. If she got lost, she wasn't ever going to find him!

Panicking, she ran in the direction she had come from, looking for the door. All she saw were reflections of herself.

Suddenly she froze. She had the distinct feeling that someone was following her. Though she didn't hear anything, the hair on the back of her neck stood up. Was it Elijah – with his club? She had to get out of there!

McKenzie began to turn in a slow circle, her body tensed, ready to spring.

Something tapped her on the back.

She was too frightened to scream. She ducked to the right, slipping beneath an arm.

Whoever it was growled in frustration and pounded after her with heavy steps.

Following her instincts, McKenzie took off again to the left, her hands slapping against the mirrors, running faster than she ever had in her life. Suddenly, the mirrors were gone. She was out of the Hall and in a new room in the Fun House – a giant barrel that was, to her relief, not turning. She saw a red light beyond the barrel – the Exit sign! She ran toward it to a heavy metal door. She pushed it open and raced outside.

She was out of the Fun House at last. Fresh evening air had never smelled so good. She stood for a moment, breathing hard, trying to calm herself. She looked around the darkened park. Most of the workers had gone home, apparently. Idlewood was deserted, and she had to get help. She had to find Tony or someone who would call the police. Jimmy needed help – fast!

She ran toward the little trailer park and stopped, not sure which one belonged to Tony.

She opened her mouth to call for help when the door to Dinah's trailer swung open. The Fat Lady stood on the threshold, her eyes glinting. 'Come in, Miss Gold,' she said. 'I've been expecting you.'

CHAPTER 16

As McKenzie stared at Dinah's huge form outlined against the doorway of the trailer, a feeling of dread swept over her. She knew that the woman was dangerous; she also knew that Dinah was the key to finding her brother.

She followed as Dinah stepped back into the trailer. It took her eyes a moment to adjust. The trailer was dark and clouded with incense. She could just make out Dinah at one end of the narrow room. The woman sat on a bench, facing what appeared to be a small altar. Her back was turned to McKenzie.

'Where's my brother?' McKenzie demanded.

The Fat Lady shrugged, her eyes gazing into a mirror that lay on the altar. 'I don't have him.'

McKenzie stood behind Dinah, resisting the

urge to grab her by the throat. 'Tell me where he is!'

'You don't need me to tell you, Miss Gold. You can figure it out for yourself.' Her eyes narrowed. 'Think hard. Where is he?'

McKenzie closed her eyes. Jimmy's voice echoed plaintively in her mind, calling her name. At first he sounded just the way he had in the Hall of Mirrors. Then McKenzie realized there was more of an echo in his voice. As if he was in a larger, more cavernous place – 'The Catacombs!'

Dinah heaved herself to her feet, and stepped toward McKenzie. 'I warned you. Now – '

McKenzie didn't listen to the rest. She ran through the open door and back to the midway, all the way to the rear of the park.

She stopped dead outside the Catacombs. Faint shouts echoed from somewhere inside the tunnels. The ticket taker was gone, but the door behind the entrance gate was open.

She knew she had to find her way back to the alcove she'd discovered when she got separated from Aidan and Lilicat. The one where she'd had the vision of being strangled. That's where she would find her brother.

She stepped in, the damp, cloying smell of the tunnels closing around her. She wished she

147

had a flashlight. All the lights were off in the tunnels. She felt her way along the rough, gritty walls with her hands. At least no holograms would be jumping out at her tonight.

She retraced the route she'd taken with her friends as well as she could. Finding the first alcove was no problem. McKenzie groped around in the dark, tapping on rocks, looking for the papier-mâché one that covered the hidden lever.

She found it. Bracing herself, she pulled the lever that opened the chute. She plummeted down, landing on the padded mat at the bottom.

This was the room where that hairy thing had approached them, sniffing. The room felt empty now. She could make out an archway in the darkness and she hurried toward that.

Up ahead someone called her name. For a second her heart leapt into her throat. Was that Jimmy calling her? Or the creature that lived here – the spirit of the miner?

Slowly, she moved along the narrow corridor, holding a hand out to either side to guide herself.

The ceiling got lower and lower, pressing her down until she had to crawl. The whole world seemed to have gone dark. Tiny bits of rock fell into her hair as her head brushed against the ceiling. The tunnel pressed in on either side.

She reached the dead end. She felt the air get cooler, as she had before, and knew that here she could stand. She slowly got to her feet.

She was somewhere near the altar room. She could sense it and yet she couldn't really tell where it was.

She heard a thumping sound coming from the side. Was that the altar room? She pushed where she thought the door should be, and her fingers met solid rock. Maybe it was farther to the right. Using her hands, she continued to push against the damp stone. Finally, with a low groaning sound, the door swung open.

McKenzie felt a wave of terror sweep through her as she saw the flaring torches and the altar made of rocks. She forced herself to step forward, her eyes searching the shadows for a sign of her brother.

'Jimmy?' Her voice came out in a broken whisper. 'Jim –' She never even finished the word. A long-fingered arm shot out and closed hard around her throat.

CHAPTER 17

McKenzie tried to pull the hand away from her throat, but it tightened around her.

'Stretchman!' she choked out. The tall man's eyes were glazed, almost as if he didn't really see her.

McKenzie twisted out of his grasp as Stretchman reached one long arm out to shut the door.

She ran for the door, but she wasn't fast enough. It shut with an ominous thud.

McKenzie turned to face him, trying to sense what she could about the giant who loomed before her in the torchlight. Of all the freaks, he had always seemed the gentlest, the one least likely to hurt anyone.

'Stretchman, please!' He backed her toward the altar, as if he didn't hear her. And she realized that he probably didn't. He was

moving like someone under hypnosis. He was
under someone else's power. Dinah's!

He reached for her.

'You don't want to hurt me, do you?'
McKenzie cried.

Stretch's eyes flickered. Still, he took another
step toward her.

McKenzie thought frantically. There had to
be a signal that would snap him out of this.
She tried snapping her fingers and clapping her
hands. She tried counting and using phrases
like 'Wake up!' None of it worked.

Calm down, she told herself, think ration-
ally.

She knew from experience that even under
hypnosis a person won't do anything against
his will. Hoping that was true, she tried again.
'You don't really want to hurt me, do you?
You're not a killer, Stretchman. Don't let
Dinah turn you into one.'

The words had no effect on the giant. He
moved toward her, lumbering but deliberate.
McKenzie couldn't remember ever having felt
so frightened.

But McKenzie's own words stayed with her.
Dinah had done this to him with her power.
Maybe McKenzie could undo the hypnosis
with *her* power.

She concentrated on Stretchman, trying to feel whatever it was he was feeling. Fear threatened to strangle her. Then it hit her – Dinah had scared him to death. Stretchman felt like a trapped animal, and he was willing to fight anything in his way to survive. McKenzie knew she had to soothe him. First she calmed herself. Then she tried to send calm and warmth to him.

The tall man seemed to relax a little. He stopped where he was, long arms dangling at his sides.

'It's all right,' McKenzie said, trying to keep her voice from shaking. 'No one's going to hurt you.'

Stretchman blinked. He seemed to be listening to her now, but McKenzie couldn't be sure he'd help her. 'There's nothing to be afraid of,' she reassured him.

Stretch looked around him, and pure terror crossed his face. 'We've got to get out of here!' he said.

'First tell me where my brother is,' said McKenzie. 'Where's Jimmy?'

Stretchman ignored her. He was at the door to the altar room, trying desperately to pull it open.

McKenzie wedged herself between him and

the door. 'Will you please tell me what's going on?'

For the first time, Stretchman really looked at her. 'You already know,' he said, his voice trembling, as if he were afraid for his life. 'This place is haunted by the spirit of a miner who died here years ago. He's become a monster. He feeds on the living. All this time Dinah's kept him away from us. No one besides us knew about him until you.'

'And so she lured me down here?' McKenzie guessed. 'Dinah's decided I'm the one who should be his next meal?'

Stretch nodded. 'We've got to get out of here,' he repeated.

'What about Jimmy?'

'The little boy. He's safe.' The tall man glanced around him fearfully.

'But how do you know for sure?' McKenzie wailed. 'What do we do now?'

The first thing we do is get out of here. We're trapped in here with the miner. We've got to get out!'

CHAPTER 18

'**I can't get** this open!' Stretchman cried, still struggling with the door.

'There's another one in here somewhere,' McKenzie said. 'It's the way I got out last time.'

She searched the walls, looking for the hidden door, and finally found it. Working together, they managed to push the stone door open. Then Stretchman led the way through the Catacombs.

McKenzie followed the giant through the maze of shadowy corridors. He was taking a different route than she'd taken with Aidan and Lilicat. It led downhill and then further downhill, so deep into the earth she wondered if they'd ever get out.

And then suddenly they were on the rocky shelf above the chasm. Torches burned on the wall beside them. Work lights from the tunnel across the chasm threw off a feeble glare. Below them the rope bridge swayed, as if being rocked by the wind. McKenzie's stomach knotted tight.

Stretchman came to a halt. 'We have to cross it,' he told McKenzie, sounding even more frightened than she was.

McKenzie peered over the edge and bit down on her lip. On either side of the bridge the abyss plunged into darkness. She clutched her stomach.

Lurching footsteps sounded behind them. 'The miner!' Stretchman said.

McKenzie's heart contracted in terror. She really was going to have to cross the bridge again.

She set her right foot on the bridge and then took two brave steps. Stretchman was right behind her, so close she could feel his breath in her hair. Don't look down, she repeated to herself. Don't look down. She took another step and another.

Dinah's harsh, familiar voice rasped behind them. 'That's right, Miss Gold. Out to the center of the bridge and then over. He's waiting for you below in the abyss.'

McKenzie and Stretchman turned around.

Dinah stood on the ledge they'd just left. Her footsteps were the ones they'd heard. The bridge swayed. McKenzie gripped the side tighter, weak with nausea.

'As for you, Stretchman, I have others who are more reliable, who won't betray me. Since you're so fond of the girl, you can join her. I'm sure He'll enjoy gnawing on your bones.'

Stretchman's mouth opened, but no words came out.

'Come on,' McKenzie whispered. 'It's not far. We can make it across.'

She turned her back to Dinah and began to walk. She'd made it before. She could make it again.

Suddenly, the bridge shook violently. On the other side, Elijah was hacking away at the ropes with a long, curved knife. One of the ropes was frayed, nearly severed.

Shorty, Madame Beaupree, and one or two others cringed behind Elijah. Shorty's face wore an expression of anguish as he stared at his friend Stretch.

McKenzie was trapped. Elijah and his knife on one side of the bridge. Dinah on the other! She couldn't run. If she was going to save their lives, she'd have to try something else. She turned to look at Dinah, then poured her energy into reading the woman's thoughts.

Dinah's mind was as securely locked as a fortress.

Elijah kept hacking away at the rope. McKenzie tried again, reaching out for Dinah's mind, searching for a weak spot. But instead of weakness, she felt Dinah's psychic energy battering against her own.

McKenzie froze. Dinah's power was strong, malevolent, almost impossible to resist. Still gripping the ropes, she sank to her knees. Would this be the end? Her friends and family passed through her mind. Lilicat. Aidan. Her parents. Jimmy.

And she felt something surge through her, giving her strength.

'You can't fight me,' Dinah said. 'You think you have a gift. What good is it doing you now?' She stared at McKenzie, who clutched the crippled bridge. 'I know what's in your mind. Fear. Anger. Confusion. Isn't that right?'

No, thought McKenzie. You're wrong. The people I love are with me. Helping me. She visualized them again, one at a time. Lilicat. Aidan. Her parents. Jimmy. And with each of their faces came more strength. More energy.

She got to her feet and turned to face Dinah

again. She channeled all her thoughts toward Dinah. This time she broke through the woman's psychic barrier.

A look of shock crossed the Fat Lady's face. 'Don't think you've won yet, McKenzie Gold.'

McKenzie glanced behind her at the freaks on the other side of the abyss. Elijah had stopped cutting the rope. He dropped his knife and pointed beyond McKenzie in Dinah's direction.

McKenzie gasped. Behind Dinah, a cleft in the rock wall slowly opened. And something hideous stepped through.

CHAPTER 19

'**Cut the rope**, Elijah!' Dinah ordered. 'He's hungry! He's waiting!'

The thing leered over Dinah's shoulder into the dim cavern, its lipless mouth revealing blackened gums and rotted teeth.

Horror washed over McKenzie like a cold wave – and Dinah felt it. The Fat Lady froze. She knew He stood behind her, but she couldn't help turning to look. And when she did, she lost all composure. She quivered violently, her strength melted by fear. The creature moved toward her. Dinah took a step back – toward the edge of the rocky shelf.

The other freaks screamed and scurried away through the passage on the other side that led to safety. McKenzie saw that the bridge was now held by only a thread. But they had to cross.

She grabbed Stretch by the arm. 'Come on, let's go!' she shouted.

The two of them turned and ran, just making it off the bridge before it tore away and dropped into the chasm.

Stretchman kept going through the same passage the other freaks had taken, but McKenzie stopped and turned to look back just before she reached the top of the passageway. Dinah was poised on the edge of the abyss. The miner reached out his arm and rested a rotting hand on her shoulder.

Dinah's eyes widened with horror. McKenzie cringed as the miner slowly advanced toward Dinah, his mouth open in a toothless gape. The fat woman stepped back over the ledge, wheezing in panic, struggling to find a foothold. For a moment she balanced on one leg and tried to clutch at the monster to keep from falling . . . but her hands slid over his oozing body and she fell backward. With a look of horrified disbelief she tumbled into the abyss. Dinah's tortured screams rang through the chasm. McKenzie buried her face in her hands and opened – her eyes in time to see the grotesque, decaying figure of the miner leaping hungrily after Dinah, his cruel laugh echoing throughout the cavern.

CHAPTER 20

Feeling sick to her stomach, McKenzie turned and followed Stretch up the passage. The tall man ran hunched over to avoid hitting his head. He stopped so suddenly McKenzie almost plowed into him.

'Your brother.' He pressed a hidden lever and a door sprang open.

Jimmy crouched against the far back wall, staring at Stretch with wide eyes. When he saw McKenzie, he dove into her arms.

'You can do that later,' Stretch said, pushing them ahead of him. 'We can't stay in here. He might come back!'

Stretch led them out of the cavern and back onto the midway, where McKenzie hugged her brother, breathing deeply in the cool night air. She could still smell the dankness of the Cata-

combs in her clothes and hair. She wondered if
that odor would ever wash out.

'How did you wind up here tonight?' she
asked Jimmy.

'Brian's older brother, Richard, took us,' he
answered. 'Mom and Dad said it was okay. But
then I got separated from Brian and Richard in
the Hall of Mirrors.' His face was grimy and
tear-stained, McKenzie saw.

'We'd better call Mom and let them know
you're all right,' she said. 'Then I've got to call
the police.'

With her arm around Jimmy, McKenzie
began to walk toward the public phones She
stopped when she saw the freaks, huddled in a
group, watching her. 'What is it?' she asked.

'Are you going to tell anyone what happened
in there?' Stretch asked fearfully. 'Like the
police?'

McKenzie sighed. 'Of course. I have to. That
creature – the miner – he's going to kill again.'

'No one will believe there's a monster in
there,' Shorty said. 'Let us take care of it. We
give you our word no one else will get hurt.'

'Mack,' Jimmy said, 'I want to go home.' His
voice shook. McKenzie could tell he was still
scared half to death.

The first thing she had to do was get him out

of Idlewood. 'Okay,' McKenzie told her brother, 'let's go.'

Once they were out of the park, she stopped to use a pay phone. She called information for the number of the Barrington police, then called the station and asked to speak with Officer Rizzuto.

'There's been a bad accident at Idlewood,' she told the policewoman. 'In the Catacombs. You should go there – it's related to the girl who almost drowned. I've got to take my brother home, but I promise to give you a complete statement first thing in the morning.'

As she drove Jimmy home, McKenzie heard the wail of police sirens approaching the park. She looked down at her brother, who had fallen asleep beside her. If only they could trade places. She was so exhausted, it was all she could do to keep her eyes open.

Early the next morning, McKenzie was awakened by the shrill ringing of the phone. Stumbling out into the hall, she picked it up on the seventh ring.

'It's me,' Lilicat announced.

'Good morning, you,' McKenzie replied sleepily. Even half-asleep, she smiled. It was a lazy summer morning, and she was starting her day with a phone call from Lilicat. Life was back to normal.

'Mack, listen,' Lilicat went on in a rush. 'Tony and I were supposed to go to the Extreme Dream concert tonight, but the most awful thing happened. There was a terrible fire at the park. The Catacombs is destroyed – burned to the ground. All of Tony's hard work was for nothing! They're going to close down Idlewood for a month at least. And you'll never guess what else!'

McKenzie didn't have to guess. She already knew what her friend was going to say.

'The freaks. They're all gone. They hitched up their trailers and just disappeared. Tony doesn't understand how they could just leave like that, unless they were the ones who set the fire. But why would they do a thing like that?'

McKenzie knew why. She told Lilicat apologetically that she'd speak to her later, hung up, and punched in the number of the Barrington police department.

'Officer Rizzuto,' she said, 'I've got a lot to tell you . . .'

EPILOGUE

Idlewood Park, some time in the future

The sandy-haired man in the tan business suit stood in the deserted amusement park, gazing at the blackened, boarded-up wooden structure. 'What do you think this is?' he asked his partner.

The shorter man beside him referred to his blueprint, and shrugged. 'One of the rides. Looks like it was boarded up after a fire. Doesn't say here what it was called.'

'Whatever it was, it was big,' said the man in the tan suit. 'It's got me curious.'

His partner stuck a pencil behind his ear. 'I'll have the crews start tomorrow. They can look at what's left of the rides, see what it'll take to get this place up and running again.'

'The first thing we'll do is see what's inside this wooden thing. Have the workmen pull the boards and all that steel off. I'm going in.'

From the depths of the Catacombs, far below, there came a chuckle, as if something inside were alive. . . .

McKenzie Gold. She's young, she's psychic, she's got

THE POWER

Share more of her terrifying experiences in

AIDAN'S FATE

'Aidan,' she said. 'It's going to happen on Valentine's Day.' She explained about the dee-jay.

'Okay,' said Aidan. 'So what's going to happen on Valentine's Day?'

She didn't answer. She couldn't speak the words: 'You're going to die.'

The darkness in Aidan's eyes told her he understood. He worriedly rubbed the crooked bump on his nose. 'When's Valentine's Day?'

'Uh . . . February fourteenth, which is . . .'

'A week from this Thursday.'

McKenzie didn't know who would want to hurt Aidan. But she knew this. They now had less than two weeks to change Aidan's fate.

Meet McKenzie Gold. She's smart, pretty – and psychic!
she's got

Red Fox are proud to present six seriously
spine-chilling adventures of Mack and her
friends . . . and her visions. Join them in our
new horror series as Mack's supernatural
powers are often stretched to their limit.
Decide for yourself – is it a gift or a curse?

The Possession
ISBN 0099220911   £2.99

The Witness
ISBN 0099221012   £2.99

The Fear Experience
ISBN 009922111X   £2.99

The Diary
ISBN 0099221217   £2.99

Aidan's Fate
ISBN 0099221314   £2.99

The Catacombs
ISBN 0099221411   £2.99

Haunting a book shop near you!